I0450978

ROCKED AND BOTHERED

A GRACEFALL ROCK STAR ROMANCE

VICTORIA ZAK

Sign up for Victoria Zak's newsletter on her website to
receive a free ebook copy of her
Guardians of Scotland novella
Highland Destiny

You'll also find additional special offers, bonus content and
info on new releases.

www.victoriazakromance.com
victoria@victoriazakromance.com

facebook.com/VictoriaZakAuthor

bookbub.com/authors/victoria-zak

instagram.com/victoriazakromance

twitter.com/VictoriaZak2

Rocked and Bothered: A Gracefall Rock Star Romance
Victoria Zak
Copyright 2022 by Victoria Zak

All rights reserved. Except as permitted under the U.S. Copyright Act 1976, no part of this publication may be reproduced, distributed, or transmitted in any form or by any means, or stored in a database or retrieval system without prior written permission of the author and publisher.

All characters, events, and locations in this book are fictitious. Any similarity to real persons, dead or living, is coincidental and not intended by the author.

Cover Design by JAB Designs

ISBN: 978-1-942516-39-2

Created with Vellum

This series is dedicated to the wild at heart. Rock on!

A new year, a new Dylan Grace. The twelve-step recovery program wasn't so bad. He'd done it, was released a few days ago, and was now home lying naked on his bed with a familiar, beautiful redhead's lips wrapped around his dick. Ashley Monroe. Silently, he sighed. Talk about toxic.

When he'd invited his ex-girlfriend over, his intentions had been innocent. Following the recovery steps, he'd needed to ask for forgiveness for being a douchebag to her from the day they had met. There was something about being honest that had turned them both on, and they'd ended up fucking.

Dylan closed his eyes. He wasn't in love with Ash like he'd been before he entered rehab. He knew that now, as there were no feelings of love, just pure, raw pleasure. Yeah, she had torn him apart when she'd started dating his band manager, Davidson. Anger and rage had been the only way he'd known how to deal with a broken heart.

He couldn't lie; he wished Davidson was here right now watching them. A sly grin formed across Dylan's lips.

Sticking it to Davidson felt good...damn good. Fuck yeah, dude, what he wouldn't do to see Davidson's face right now.

Yet, Dylan wouldn't say a word. Davidson not only managed Gracefall, but he managed Ash's band, Blushing Alice. Besides, he was about healing not revenge. He was no longer part of her life to the level he could tell her who to date.

"Ash," he moaned as he fisted her hair. Christ, she felt awesome. His thoughts were clear but raced at the same time. Dylan looked down and caught a glimpse of Ash's face bobbing up and down on his cock. She glanced up and winked. *Fuck!*

His body stiffened. He didn't know if it was Ash's mad blow job skills or being celibate for ninety days, but he came hard and fast. Stars bursting behind his eyes and all.

Ash slinked up his body licking her lips. "Just like I remembered."

As Dylan tried to reclaim part of his soul, he nodded.

She rolled onto her side and played with his nipple piercing. "You're a beautiful man, Dylan Grace."

He opened his eyes to Ash's wicked smile. She bit her bottom lip as his gaze met hers. Fuck, she had that look— the look that could bring him to his knees.

No. Fucking. Way. Not doing that.

"It's just sex, Ash." Dylan sat up and rolled out of bed. He grabbed his jeans and put them on. "Besides, you're with Davidson."

"I know." Ash covered her body with the sheet. "I thought since we're wiping the slate clean, I could be honest. Guess I was wrong,"

Dylan saw the hurt in her eyes. "Shit." He scrubbed his short blond hair, still getting used to the new length. He sat down on the edge of the bed, feeling like an asshole. "I'm sorry, Ash. I can't go back to the way things were."

"I can't either. I'm ready to move on, but something is stopping me. I need to know that we're okay. I can't lose you as a friend."

Dylan reached over and held her hand. "Same here. I want us to be friends. I can accept that you're with Davidson even though he's an asshole."

"Stop." She swatted him playfully. "He's been good to me."

Dylan nodded but highly doubted that was true. Hey, they say love is blind. "So, we're friends," Dylan confirmed.

"Absolutely."

"Friends with benefits?" He gazed at Ash with a raised brow.

"You're pushing it, Grace," Ash teased as she got out of bed.

"I'm just checking. It's important to know your boundaries." As Dylan sat on the edge of the bed, he watched Ash wiggle into her tight jeans.

They had never been truly happy. How could they when they were both fucked up emotionally? When he'd first met Ash, she'd been a way to pay his bills so he could chase his dream of becoming a rock star. But when Ash began to pursue her singing career, he'd become jealous. Jealous that her band had rapidly become successful, but also selfish because he'd had to share her with the world. There'd only been room for one egomaniac in their relationship, and it had to be him.

He'd been a jealous, selfish, emotionally numb fucker. It had only taken ninety days of therapy to recognize it.

"Grace, take care of yourself."

The sincerity of her words cut him profoundly. He didn't deserve her forgiveness.

Before he drowned in self-loathing, Dylan brushed off the past and locked that fucking door. "Yeah." He scrubbed his hands through his hair. "No need to worry. I'm good. Going to start working on some new material so I can get back on the road. I need that."

"Don't push yourself too hard. You don't want to relapse."

Dylan read through her heartfelt words of wisdom—what she was really saying was "when would Dylan Grace slip back into his old ways?" It frustrated him that she didn't believe in him. Then again, why should Ash? He'd broken that trust. Yeah, she might have forgiven him, but she hadn't forgotten.

Baby steps, Dylan reminded himself. Indeed, he was a work in progress, and he had a lot of work to do to regain trust with Ash and the band.

The truth was he wasn't strong, not like his brother, Joe. His addiction was a relentless, colossal beast that would be hard to beat. That fucker had an army of demons on its side, constantly testing Dylan's mental fortitude. All his life, those demons danced on his self-worth, reminding him that he wasn't good enough. No matter how much fortune and fame he had, Dylan would always be the poor, dirty trailer park kid whose mom loved drugs more than her sons.

The battle had started ninety days ago, and Dylan already felt exhausted, which scared him. If the monster was victorious, he'd end up dead, and he didn't want to be a rocker cliché.

Dylan inhaled, in with the good air, out with the bad. The last thing he wanted to do was to dump his baggage on Ash. That's why he had a therapist. "Seriously, Ash, it's all good." He put on his best fake smile, which she believed. He was a master at hiding his emotions.

"Good." Ash walked toward the door, and before she opened it, she turned to Dylan. "If you need me, you know where to find me." Dylan nodded. Ash opened the door and took a step out, then paused. "Um, you have company."

Dylan's head popped up. "Shit!" He'd forgotten about the two p.m. band meeting. He rushed around, looking for a shirt. "Sorry about that." Dylan found a black T-shirt on the floor by the bed. He picked it up, gave it a good sniff, then put it on.

"Nothing like doing the walk of shame in front of your friends." Ash shrugged and proceeded out of the bedroom to the front door. He heard Tyler and Joe say goodbye to Ash.

Fuck, the guys were all here. And fuck, didn't anyone know how to knock? Dylan whipped out his phone and wrote into his notes app to change the locks ASAP.

Dylan walked out of his bedroom, acting like nothing had happened. "Hey, guys."

"What the fuck was that?" Joe stared at him from the sofa with his mouth wide open.

"Joe, that's none of our business." Melody, Joe's fiancée, sat next to him, looking just as shocked.

"It's totally my business. Ash is dating our band manager." Joe gave Dylan an *I don't get you, bro* glare. "This isn't going to work." Joe stood. "I'm fucking out of here."

"Wait." Jake, one of the band's guitarist, stopped the drummer in his tracks. "The meeting hasn't started yet. We don't know why Ash was here, and does it really matter?"

"Fuck yeah, dude." Dylan fist-bumped Jake. "I knew you'd have my back."

Jake glared at him. "Don't push it a-hole."

"Right." Dylan shoved his hands in the front pockets of his Levis. "Look, if you want to know why Ash was here, all you have to do is ask."

"No!" everyone in the room yelled.

"No need for details," Tyler, the bassist, said as he reclined in Dylan's leopard-print chaise lounge, causing Dylan to cringe.

"Dude, feet." Dylan slapped Tyler's combat boots off the furniture.

"Can we all stop beating around the bush?" Elliot, Jake's girlfriend and Gracefall's rhythm and lead guitarist, said, looking frustrated.

"I think Dylan beat us to it," Tyler snickered.

"Oh, for Christ's sake." Elliot shook her head.

"Okay, that's enough." Joe sat back down. "Elliot's right. Let's start the meeting."

Dylan grabbed a chair from out of the kitchen. He spun it around, then straddled it, folding his arms and resting them on the back. He knew what was on everyone's mind: *When will he fuck up?* "I'm all ears."

Joe cleared his throat. "Next week, we're in the studio working on material for the new album, then we're preparing for the tour, then back on the road, and then there's whatever pops up in between." Joe looked at Dylan, and this little bro picked up what he was putting down. "Dylan, the next few months are going to be stressful. You can't fuck this up."

Yep, he'd called it. "Wow, bro, I didn't know you cared so much." Dylan teased, but there was truth behind it. The last time he'd seen Joe was the first and last time he'd visited him in rehab. He remembered it clearly.

There were heavy glares.

"How could you be so stupid, Dylan?" he'd said.

There were flaring nostrils.

"Didn't you learn what not to do from Karen?" *Like mother like son, the apple didn't fall far from the tree.*

"You're breaking up the band."

There was shouting, storming out of the room, and slamming doors in more ways than one—Joe was closed off, still angry with him. Big bro had taken his addiction like a slap in the face. As a young boy, Joe had been forced to grow up fast. Looking back, Dylan realized how much his brother had sacrificed for him. Joe had given up his childhood to take care of him, which weighed heavily on Dylan's heart.

So yeah, becoming a drug addict after Joe had done everything to keep him on the straight and narrow, Dylan understood the betrayal Joe felt but didn't know how to fix it. Or was it too late?

Joe's jaw clenched as he pointed at Dylan, obviously not appreciating his sarcasm. "Listen, you little shit—"

"I think what Joe is trying to say is," Melody gave Joe the *cool your shit or else* look, "we want you to stay on course with your recovery and stay healthy."

"Mel is right," Elliot added. "Stress is a trigger that may entice you to use again, and we don't want to put you in a predicament that will jeopardize your recovery efforts."

Elliot was his sponsor and thank fuck that she was. She put everything into perspective. So, when she was concerned...he listened.

"What are you saying? Are you replacing me in the band?" Dylan's heart raced as he tamped down the urge to break out in a rage. This couldn't be happening. "I'm not fragile. Stress is not going to break me."

"That's not what we're saying." Tyler sat up. "We're not replacing you. We need a plan to keep you healthy because, bro, I'm not burying another band member."

Fuck, he missed Mox. His heart still ached like it had been yesterday that they had lost their lead guitarist in a tragic bus accident over a year ago. No one in the band had dealt with Mox's death. T was drinking more, and Joe...he didn't talk about losing his best friend.

Dylan swallowed hard as he saw the grim expression on everyone's faces. He didn't want to die; he just wanted the pain to disappear. "Dude." Dylan brushed it off. "I'm not going to die. You know those KISS caskets are crazy expensive."

"KISS has a line of coffins?" Tyler asked as he pulled out his phone.

"Fuck yeah, dude." Dylan scooted closer as they searched KISS caskets online. "That one with all four original members of the band painted on top."

"Fucking sweet," Tyler awed.

"Can we get serious here?" Joe exclaimed, and Tyler put the phone down. "I'm not playing, Dylan. If you can't keep your shit together, you're out."

The room fell silent. Joe's words stung like a dagger in the heart. The thought of Joe even thinking about replacing him hurt more than anything. Gracefall was nothing without him. Dylan glared at his brother. "Why don't you stop threatening and do it?"

Joe clenched his fists; Dylan had called his bluff.

His brother turned to Melody. "I can't fucking do this. I'm going to kill him."

"Sweetheart, murder isn't the answer here." Melody rubbed Joe's arm.

"No one wants you gone, bro," Jake said. "All we want is to see you healthy."

"I'm ninety days clean," Dylan added.

"That's great and all," Elliot said. "Trust me, coming

from a recovering addict and your sponsor, it's only the beginning."

"E, don't you think I know that?" Dylan glanced at his bandmates. The same look of uncertainty was set on their faces. "I'm doing my best here. Seriously, I haven't kicked Joe's ass yet."

"You wish, fucker." Joe glared.

"Well, on that note, I appreciate everyone's concern, but it's time y'all got the fuck out of my apartment." Dylan stood and began walking toward the door.

"We're not done," Jake said.

"Wait, I want to be the one to tell him," Joe interrupted.

Dylan sat back down. This shit was getting irritating; he couldn't wait to hear this one. Were they hiring extra security to follow him around and slap drinks out of his hand?

Jake motioned for Joe to take over. "We've hired a live-in life coach for you for the time we'll be in TN, recording the next album."

"What. The. Fuck." Dylan's mouth laid open. What the hell was going on?

Joe continued. "She'll help you develop new and healthy behaviors, set goals—"

"I don't need that bullshit," Dylan grumbled. "I'm a big boy, and I can do that myself."

Joe ignored Dylan. "She'll hold you accountable for your actions."

Dylan looked at Elliot. "Elliot's my sponsor, and it's been working, right E?"

Elliot nodded. "But I'm not a life coach. Besides, don't you want someone who will encourage self-discovery and growth?"

"Oh, you guys are so full of shit," Dylan huffed. He was beyond angry. To keep his cool, he turned his head and looked out the window. Below him was Sunset Strip. Many rock stars had made names for themselves here, which made him wonder whether they had had life coaches to help stay clean.

No! This was fucking rock and roll!

He didn't need a glorified babysitter. The goal had been set: play rock and roll. He didn't need his whole life analyzed by some hag probing his brain, asking him questions about his mother, the physical abuse he'd endured from her boyfriend, or his anger issues. Besides, the last psychologist at the clinic, and there had been many, pushed too hard and ended up with their office chair thrown against the wall.

Fuck all that. He didn't have anger issues; he was tired of listening to pompous assholes spew their bullshit about what was best for him. What the fuck did they know? They didn't know him.

"We're not asking, Dylan," Tyler said. "This is going to happen."

"We care about you." Melody sat on the edge of the sofa. She leaned in and held his hand. "We all love you."

Jake did the same and laid his hand on top of Melody's. "You scared the shit out of us."

"We won't let you become another rocker cliché." Elliot placed her hand on top of Jake's.

"Yeah, what she said." Tyler smiled as he walked over. He bent down and added his hand to the pile. "Look what you've done, asshole. You got me down on one knee."

They laughed as Joe was the last member to join in on the mound of hands.

The brothers locked eyes. There were no words but an understanding that he had Joe's support.

Dylan scanned the faces of his bandmates. Something

eased inside him. They were his family, and they truly loved him. What could it hurt to go along with the plan? One night alone with Dylan Grace and he'd have the hag running for her life. So, yeah, bring on the life coach.

"So, who is this life coach?"

"Dani," Joe answered.

"What?" Melody exclaimed, followed by Dylan. The hand pyramid crumbled.

"You mean Dani as in Mellie's best friend?" Dylan prayed it wasn't so.

"Yes," Joe said.

"No!" Melody shook her head. "No way. Not happening."

"I happen to agree," Dylan added.

"We talked to her before coming over, and she accepted the job." Joe looked at his fiancée. "I don't see the problem. We can trust her to act in Dylan's best interest. She already knows him, and she won't go public with this information."

"Joe, you don't understand what you've done," Melody said.

"Melody, no disrespect." Tyler sat back down and moved far away from Melody's reach. "But technically, this isn't your decision. It's band business."

Melody shot Tyler a glare. "She's my best friend, and that makes it my business." She turned back to Joe. "I can't believe you." Melody stormed out of Dylan's apartment.

"Mel, wait!" Joe followed her outside.

How could they think that hiring Dani, the woman he'd fucked on and off with no strings attached for the past five years, would be a good idea? Dylan smiled. Maybe this wasn't so bad after all.

Dani was gorgeous and, most of all, he liked her. This could be fun.

"By the way," Jake added as everyone was racing out of

the apartment, "don't kill the messenger. No sex while we're in TN."

Dylan shot him a confused glare. "Wait—"

"Yeah, we don't want one addiction to turn into another addiction." The guy who Dylan thought had his back ran out the door quickly.

"This isn't over," Dylan yelled from the door. "No sex? Come on, guys!"

2

*D*ani sat at the local café waiting for her best friend, Melody, to show for lunch. Along with Melody's mother, she had spent all morning at an upscale bridal shop in Beverly Hills helping Melody pick the perfect wedding dress. Dani had zipped, tucked, and fluffed Melody into at least twenty different dresses before the perfect one appeared.

She recalled the exact moment the magic occurred. Melody had been standing on a pale pink dais in front of a three-way mirror admiring the elegant ivory lace Boho wedding dress when her mother began to cry. The gown had hugged her every curve. Dani had been speechless as she imaged how stunning her best friend would look under the sunset on the beach as Melody married the man of her dreams.

However, there had been tension between the two of them, and Dani knew exactly what it was about. She couldn't believe it either. Why had she agreed to be Dylan Grace's life coach? Was she insane?

"Hey," Melody greeted her in a whirlwind. "I'm so sorry

I'm late. My mom has been driving me crazy." She sat across from Dani and opened the menu. "I think my parents are trying to get back together."

"Really?" Dani was shocked. "After all these years of fighting?" Melody's parents had gone through a horrible and public divorce and, through the years, had made Melody's life a living hell.

"Yeah, ever since the engagement party they have been on good terms."

"So, how do you feel about that?"

Melody put down the menu and folded her arms on the table. "Okay, I'm tired of pretending nothing is wrong, and I'm just going to come out and say it. Why did you agree to be Dylan's life coach?"

Dani had been wondering when this conversation would come up. "Because I care and want to help."

"Knowing your history with Dylan, do you think this is a good decision? What about your master's degree? Since I've known you, you've wanted to be a psychologist."

"I can take some classes online—"

"It's not the same. Besides, Dylan is a full-time job. Twenty-four seven. You won't have time for anything else."

"Mel—"

"No, Dani. He doesn't need a life coach. He needs a therapist. There are things in his past that haunt him—things he won't talk about, not even to Joe. He needs more than a cheerleader."

"Mel—"

"Have you forgotten how emotionally wrecked he leaves you? You might be a fuck buddy for him, but for you, it's different. You're not a doormat for Dylan Grace to park his boots on whenever he feels like it. I don't want to see you get hurt."

"Melody!" Dani yelled, trying to get Melody's attention.

"What?"

"Can I talk now?"

Melody exhaled. "I'm sorry. Since I found out, I've been trying to process everything."

"Making your pros and cons list." Dani smiled. Melody was notorious for her lists. She made them for everything.

"You know me so well."

"And because of that, I haven't left." Dani adjusted in her seat, ready to defend herself. "I appreciate your concern. I really do, but this is my decision. Mel, Dylan overdosed and almost died. Regardless of my feelings for him, I can't stand by and do nothing. He doesn't need another therapist psychoanalyzing him. Dylan needs positivity in his life, and with my expertise, I know I can help. Trust me. I'm not being naïve. I know what I'm doing." Well, at least she hoped she did.

"I wish I was as confident." Melody shook her head and fidgeted with the straw from her water glass. "I love Dylan, and I wish him well. I think someone else should take the job. You're too kind for Dylan Grace."

Dani couldn't understand why her best friend refused to see her side. Why didn't she trust her decision? Maybe because Dani wasn't entirely convinced herself. Melody's assessment had been spot on.

Ever since Dani had met Dylan, she'd been a victim of his rocker charm. Every time he was in town, he'd call her, and they'd hook up. On the outside looking in, Dylan used her, and she allowed it because he was a famous rock star. But it went further than that. She saw a raw side of Dylan that other people didn't see. Beyond the rocker persona, Dylan was genuine and kind, a person she loved to hate.

There was something about him that drew her in and kept her captive.

It was the moments in between, when they were alone and being honest, that Dani had fallen for Gracefall's frontman. She knew the hookup was all she was going to get, but try telling that to her heart. The aftermath of a night or two with Dylan Grace wasn't pretty. A week of going through missing him was exhausting; heartache led to thinking she'd be all right without him, which led to swearing him off. She was left wrecked, and Mel was always there to nurse her back to life. No matter how many times she denied it, Mel knew how hard she had fallen. Empty ice cream cartons scattered throughout her apartment were a dead giveaway every time.

Dani straightened. She'd made the decision, and she was sticking to it. She could help Dylan. "I know you're worried, but things have changed."

"How? How have things changed?"

"Dylan is my client. It's no longer personal."

"I hope you're right."

Dani reached across the table and held Melody's hand. "I'll be fine. I promise."

"I know you will be because I'll make sure of it."

Confusion spread across Dani's face.

"I'm going to Tennessee with Joe while they record the next album."

"Let me guess. You just decided that?"

"Yep, Joe will be thrilled that I'm tagging along. Besides, us girls have to stick together while the boys are busy. It will be fun."

Dani glared at Melody. "I see what you're doing."

"What?" Melody acted innocent, as if she had no clue what Dani was talking about.

"You don't have to spend the next few months in Tennessee waiting for me to fall apart because I can't handle Dylan Grace."

"That's not what I'm doing."

Dani cocked her head to the side giving her best friend the *yeah, right* stare down.

"Fine. I can't help it. I know what he does to you."

"Listen, you don't have to worry. When I talked to Joe about the job, he told me Dylan knew the rules. There will be no hookups, sex, whatever. I'm a professional. It's my job to make sure Dylan progresses to the next stage of his recovery. Trust me, I got this."

"It's not you I don't trust." Melody pursed his lips together. "Joe should have talked to me before hiring you."

"Don't be mad at Joe. It wouldn't have changed a thing." Dani placed her hand on top of Melody's. "We'll have fun. Manis and pedis while the boys play."

Dani watched a small smile form on her best friend's lips. "Okay."

"Yeah?"

"Yes, I trust you."

Dani was relieved that Melody had finally seen things her way or at least tried. Nothing was going to stop her from bringing balance to the rocker's life, because a world without Dylan Grace was a tragedy in itself. He was already one overdose closer to death, and she was one heartbeat away from heartache.

*a*fter a four-and-a-half-hour flight, an hour waiting to pick up her rental car, and a two-hour drive through the mountains, Dani finally arrived in Pine Mountain, Tennessee. A friendly voice coming through the vehicle's speakers informed her that the cabin's location was around the next bend. "Thank God," Dani sighed as she kept laser-focused on the road. Driving up narrow mountain roads at night wasn't for the faint of heart and certainly not for this LA girl.

Independence was a bitch. Dani had declined the limo Gracefall had sent to the airport to pick her up. First, she had wanted to experience the road trip through the mountains. Second, being stranded in the middle of nowhere with a sexy rocker who was totally off-limits wasn't a good idea. She needed a car for the next few months. God only knew when she'd need to escape Dylan Grace. Dani had never been a live-in life coach before. The small clientele she had she'd met virtually or over the phone. With being so focused on school, that was all she could handle.

Dani pulled into the driveway, passing four smaller

cabins. At the last cabin she'd passed, she saw Tyler and another guy she didn't recognize grabbing items from an old Ford pickup truck. She stopped and rolled down her window. "Nice ride, T."

"Hey, Dani." Tyler smiled and walked over to the car. He leaned in and rested his arms on the window. Good God, with all that long, curly, dark hair hanging around his chiseled-from-stone face, he looked like rock and roll heaven. Or maybe she was suffering from jet lag and lack of sleep.

"Did you just get here?"

"Yep." Tyler scratched his dark goatee. "I think you're staying in the big house."

Dani looked at the ginormous two-story log cabin in front of her. The sight took her breath away. Outside lighting cast a warm glow over the place. She couldn't see much since it was dark, but she could only imagine the stunning mountain views lying behind it. Dani couldn't wait to see inside. "Wow, looks like someone famous lives here."

Tyler grinned. "Good luck, Dani girl." He slapped the roof of her little red sportscar. "See ya around."

She needed more than luck; she needed an act of God. On the plane and in the car, she couldn't stop thinking about Dylan and the situation she'd gotten herself into. Reminiscing about their past hookups and her expectations of a no-sex, professional future warred inside her. Had she made a mistake?

No. She shook free from her self-doubt. She could handle Dylan.

Dani continued to the big house and parked in the circular driveway. Mac, Gracefall's bodyguard, and another bulky guy greeted her. "Ms. Clark, this is Gus. We'll see to your things."

What a relief. Exhausted, the last thing Dani wanted to

deal with was her luggage. However, she did pack light, considering all the winter clothes she'd had to bring, with two suitcases and a computer bag. "Thanks, guys. I appreciate it."

Dani stepped out of the car, gripping the straps of the oversized bag on her shoulder. She saw Dylan's silhouette walk past the window. Since he had been home from rehab, she hadn't heard or seen him, and when he didn't return her call after she'd accepted the job, she knew it wasn't a good sign. She had no idea how he was handling things; soon, she'd find out.

After a few deep breaths, Dani entered the cabin. Fresh pine and cinnamon lingered in the air. From the entryway she saw a beautiful spiral staircase leading to the loft. As she continued, her eyes fixated on the exposed wood beans in the ceiling, which were huge and just as beautiful as the staircase. The home was enormous, yet it felt welcoming.

Behind her, she heard her suitcases being rolled inside. "Ms. Clark, the bedrooms are upstairs past the library in the loft, and the master bedroom is yours."

Sweet, she had a freaking library to study in. Someone pinch her; she had to be dreaming. "Thank you, Mac. I'll be up in a sec to check out that library."

"Take your time. I'll leave your bags inside your room. Welcome to Pine Mountain."

And what a welcome it had been. With the elegant ambiance and the stunning views, which she knew would take her breath away once the sun came up, Dani felt like she was on vacation.

She heard someone clear their throat, bringing her attention to the living room. As she walked in, she took in the massive stone-framed fireplace and the floor-to-ceiling windows. But what took her breath away was Dylan sitting on one of the brown leather couches with one leg lazily resting over the other. Dani's heart stilled. His previous long blond mohawk was now cut short. His goatee was thicker; he was probably growing it out for winter. His leather jacket covered his tattoos, yet she could still see the ones on his hands as he held his phone, scrolling. But what she'd missed the most was those stunning blue-gray eyes that set her insides ablaze. With all his tattoos and ear piercings, the man bled rock and roll swagger.

Even though she knew him, he still had a way of intimidating her in a famous person kind of way. Nothing she couldn't handle, right? She knew a lot of famous people. But not in an intimate way like Dylan Grace.

She knew Dylan's tickle spot was his neck and that he loved to cuddle after sex in silence. Those were the brief moments Dylan let her in. Most of the time he didn't go deep into things, but his ex, Ash, had come up a little. Ash had screwed him up and was definitely one of his triggers. And it didn't help that their band manager was dating her. Metallica was his favorite band, and he'd debate with anyone that their older music was better than the newer. He enjoyed pancakes any time of day, and when she made them, she added chocolate chips because he craved his sweets. The intimate details she knew about Dylan were vast. But they were just memories.

None of that was important now. She needed to get him to reveal his past, his hurts, and all the things that had brought him to the tipping point of almost killing himself— and not really caring. To do that, Dani had already committed to observing from the outside to gain a real understanding of this man. No sex, no cuddling in bed, no orgasms for either of them.

"Hi." She walked over to the couch, and he pinned her

with a glare that stopped her dead in her tracks. He wasn't happy to see her. She was prepared for this reaction, actually expecting it.

"What the fuck, Dani?" He wasn't yelling, but the tone was every bit pissed off.

"What is that supposed to mean?"

"Don't play stupid. You're far more intelligent than that." Still, his voice was steady. Hmm, a new tactic? Was Dylan trying to challenge her, intimidate her? This should be interesting.

"Fine." Dani put her hands on her hips, reminding herself to be strong. She was trained in this sort of thing. Wasn't that what she'd been going to school for all this time? It wasn't the first time she'd put her education into practice. "Since we're playing 'Read My Mind,' I'm guessing you're not happy with my new job."

"Bingo."

"Look, Dylan, I want to help. With my expertise—"

"Don't give me that horseshit." His tone hit an octave higher. "I trusted you."

Dani was confused. "What did I do to change that, Dylan? I'm here to help you."

"If you are truly here for me, then you should have declined the job. I trusted you to do the right thing for the both of us." Dylan leaned forward, resting his elbows on his thighs. "You should have stayed the fuck away. We had a good thing going."

"Right, having sex whenever it was convenient for you. Well, time to clear the air. There will be *no* sex ."

"And what was so wrong with that?"

Everything.

Dani tamped down the urge to slap him, walk out the door, and never look back, but she wouldn't allow Dylan that satisfaction. No, he was pushing, probably with the hopes to intimidate her and get her to leave. Well, she needed to push harder. "I'm not here to climb into your bed whenever you want me. Sorry to bruise your ego, but the booty call days are over. The *only* reason I'm here is for your well-being. I don't want to see amazing talent go to waste. The world needs Dylan Grace. God help us all."

"I don't need your help. I want things like they were." Of course he did. This was his fortress, hiding his hurt behind the façade of band life and doing whatever he wanted whenever he wanted because that was what soothed his pain. The drugs, sex, attitude, it was all a cover. Her training told her it went deeper. She might be the only person who could dig deep enough into his soul to help him. This was what Dani had to nip in the bud.

Dani would be lying if she believed his words didn't faze her. They were like blades straight to her heart. "Maybe that's what you want, but you know as well as anyone they can't be like old times."

Dylan looked up. His grim expression caught her off guard. "You should have stayed away."

"Maybe I should have, but I didn't, so get over it."

"Oh, I'm so fucking over it." He leaned back and spread his arms across the back of the couch. "You're not my savior, Dani."

Heat rolled through her body. Did he really think she was that self-righteous to believe that? "I know what you're doing."

"Great!" He threw his hands in the air. "Please, psycho-analyze me. Tell me something I don't know."

Dani began to tell him but refrained. No, she would not allow him to pull her into this pissing match. "I'm going to bed." She headed toward the staircase before she lost control and told him what she was really thinking.

"It won't be long, cupcake; you'll be begging for my cock."

Dani didn't need to look back to see the smirk on his face. Her hands curled into fists as she strode upstairs. Once at the loft, she looked down to him. "Grow up, Dylan."

She heard him laugh, which only fueled her anger.

Was she really ready for Dylan Grace?

Dani strode down the hallway, stopping at the first bedroom. Thinking it was her room, she looked inside. A black duffle bag laid on the bed. Since the rest of the band was staying in the surrounding cabins, she assumed this was Dylan's room.

She continued down the hall and didn't have to go far until she reached another bedroom. This one had to be hers. Dani opened the door and she'd been right, her luggage was inside. "Great," she huffed. Of course the master bedroom would be next to Dylan's room. There was literally no way of escaping him.

The lights were dim, but Dani could make out the massiveness of the room. A king-size bed with at least three different sized pillows took up most of the room. A fireplace, which matched the stone design throughout the house, warmed the bedroom comfortably. But what she couldn't wait to see was the view from the bay window overlooking the mountain. If only the sun were up.

Dani laid her bag on the bed then made her way to the bathroom. If the bedroom looked like a posh, upscale hotel room, she could only imagine what the bathroom looked like.

Dani turned on the light. "Are you serious?" The vast garden tub framed in cedar walls and an exposed wood-beamed ceiling was an oasis. A candle-burning chandelier hung over the tub. A tray with an assortment of bath soaps, bath bombs, and oils sat on the corner of the tub. She was most definitely taking advantage of soaking in that tub.

Dani walked out of the bathroom and took in more of the bedroom. It was the most stunning bedroom she'd ever seen. She breathed in the cinnamon and pine scent, letting go of that stressful moment with Dylan. She was here to do a job, to keep Dylan Grace out of trouble. If that was even possible. He wasn't going to win.

4

*B*efore the sun was up, Dylan stood naked in the kitchen with only an apron on, beating a bowl of eggs. One thing he loved to do was cook. When he was stressed, he cooked a lot, and Dani was stressing him the fuck out.

Sometime in the early morning, Dylan's conscience had kicked in. He didn't mean to blow up on Dani like he had. No, that was a lie. He meant every word he'd said as he attempted to make her leave. The band wouldn't allow him to fire Dani, but he could sure as hell make life miserable enough that she would want to leave.

The whole life coach idea was bullshit. Any decision they made about his behavior should have included him. Who were they to make demands? And what the fuck was this no sex thing all about? The last time he checked, sex wasn't a drug. Why couldn't the guys trust him to stay clean? He hadn't given them any reason not to. He was a grown-ass man; he didn't need a babysitter, not even a hot one, watching his every move.

And that was the problem. This was Dani, the sweetest,

kindest person he knew. She was intelligent, which made him wonder why she was here in the first place. She was two kinds of beautiful: naughty and nice and way too good for rock and roll. She was the kind of person he'd end up hurting, and that's why she had to go.

Dani made him vulnerable. There was a calmness he felt being around her, like he could tell her anything, and that alone was dangerous. Revealing his demons to Dani wasn't happening. She didn't need to see the foul side of him. Fuck, even he didn't want to see it. Dylan trusted Dani with his life, but the dirty secret would stay hidden.

On top of that, having her here and not being able to touch her was the worst punishment ever. There was this electric sexual chemistry between them that he'd never felt with any other woman, and he'd been with plenty to compare. No one fucked better than Dani Clark. Fireworks and all that corny shit—she made him feel it all. How was he to keep his dick in his pants when every time he saw her he wanted to take a trip down memory lane and fuck like rabbits? When she touched him, his skin electrified and burned like a new tattoo. And her tits, her kissable, squeezable...

Fuck!

Just thinking about Dani caused his dick brain to kick in.

No. He shook his head, erasing her naked, beautiful body from his thoughts. Dani was off limits. It was best for his sobriety. This was how it had to be. Being this close to Dani would only end in disaster, and he wished she'd seen that before taking the job.

Dylan picked up his phone and texted Dani because heading to her bedroom to tell her breakfast was cooking probably wouldn't have ended well. Not after last night.

Dylan: Hey, I'm sorry. I mean, I am, and I'm not. This is difficult to process, which is no excuse to get bitchy with you. I suck.

Dylan hit send and waited impatiently for her to respond. He wouldn't blame her for not returning his text. If making her breakfast was Plan A, what was Plan B?

Dani: Do you know what time it is?

Dylan relaxed. She'd texted back. Before he could respond, Dani did.

Dani: It's six o'clock, Dylan. Six o'clock!

Dylan: I have breakfast cooking, and I've made bacon.

Dani: You're forgiven. I'll be right down.

Note to self, chicks dig bacon.

~

*D*ani quickly got out of bed. The chill in the room had her dressed in jeans, a sweater, and thick socks in record time. She pulled her hair back into a pony-tail as she thought about the night's events. It would have been naïve for her to think that Dylan wouldn't resist her help. He had a lot to take in after ninety days of rehab and coping with life sober. She didn't have time to be angry with him. They needed to talk and start their first life-coaching session.

Dani grabbed her notebook and pen, then headed downstairs to the kitchen. On the way, she went over some basic coaching questions that would ease him into difficult, soul-searching questions, where he would need to dig down deep and find out the root of his chaos. She'd seen him at his worst, which frightened her, but Dani truly believed she was the only one who could help him. It wasn't going to be easy, but she'd be beside him the entire the way.

She came to a complete stop when she saw Dylan's

naked, muscular butt peeking out from the back of his apron. He didn't notice her standing next to the kitchen island, and she didn't make herself known. Instead, she enjoyed the view for a second longer.

Dani cleared her throat, and Dylan turned around. "Morning, cupcake."

Heat rushed up her body and settled in her cheeks as his deep voice rattled her. "Morning."

Dylan went back to what he was doing, tending to something he was sautéing in a pan. "So, I was thinking about our situation and how we should deal with it."

"This is a good first step." Dani took a seat at the kitchen island.

"First, you can stay, but there will be no psychoanalyzing bullshit. I'm done with the mind-fucking."

"Agreed. I'm not here to psychoanalyze you." *Much*, she thought. That was part of the challenge before her—to help him avoid the collision course. To do that she'd need to find out his triggers. She knew some from being with him the past five years. Yes, as fuck buddies she analyzed more than Dylan knew; his performance was telling in more ways than one.

"Cool. Second, don't treat me like a juvenile delinquent. I don't need a babysitter."

"Well, don't act like one, and we won't have a problem," Dani teased.

Dylan shot her a glare. She grinned back jokingly.

He placed his hands on the counter and leaned in. Strong, lean, tattooed arms consumed Dani's thoughts as she remembered being wrapped up in those arms under the sheets. A rush of desire coursed over her body, causing her to shift in her seat. Without him even knowing it, he was wreaking havoc on her sex. Or maybe he did know.

"Third, don't look at me like that."

Embarrassed she had been caught drooling over the rock god, Dani went into complete damage control. "Like what?"

"Like you want to fuck me. Seriously, Dani, I have feelings, too," he teased as if he was offended, but that wicked smile told her another story. This was the Dylan she needed to be careful of.

"Okay." Dani gathered her thoughts away from his full pink lips. "Stop messing with me, Dylan. I really think this a positive step forward." She smiled, overjoyed that Dylan was coming around. She opened her notebook. "You need to focus on yourself and what you want in life. We need to identify what's keeping your vision from coming true. Can I ask you some goal-related questions? It will help me figure out where we need to start."

When he didn't answer, Dani looked up from her notes and saw Dylan staring at her with a crooked smile on his face. "What?"

He shook his head and chuckled. "You're cute, cupcake."

Dani huffed, feeling defeated. She thought she was getting somewhere with him. "I don't think it's very professional to be calling me cupcake."

"Dr. Cupcake?"

"I'm not a doctor yet."

"Doc Cupcake." Dylan raised his spatula. "I like it."

Dani shook her head, caving into his insanity. "Seriously, we need to set aside some time for a session."

"No can do today. After breakfast, I'm joining the guys in the studio."

"Everyone is here?"

"Joe and Mellie should be here soon. They're staying in

the cabin next to T's. Elliot and Jake got in late last night, and they're in the cabin set back in the woods."

"So, how did you get dibs on the big house?"

Dylan slid a plate of bacon toward Dani. "Because I'm the rock star." He winked, and Dani felt her insides melt. "Actually, I struck a deal. I promised to cook the meals if I could stay in the main house. I mean, look at this kitchen. It's a chef's wet dream."

All the appliances were state-of-the-art and stainless steel, and even the refrigerator was computer-operated. Black granite countertops and stone backsplash tied everything up elegantly. If she searched the cabinets, she bet she'd find one of each kitchen gadget. "Well, I'm glad you have your cooking skills to keep you busy. However, we should add in some meditation. Actually," she opened her phone to her calendar, "I'm going to schedule you in for a meditation session. I have this amazing app that will walk us through the steps. How does tomorrow sound?"

"I don't know." Dylan rubbed the back of his neck.

"How about yoga?"

"No yoga."

"Then tomorrow works for you? Bright and early?"

"You're not taking no for an answer, are you?"

"Nope."

"Well, that's not very positive. No is a negative word."

"Dylan, you're not getting out of this. Let me do my job."

"Fine."

"Good," Dani smiled in victory as she scheduled the appointment. "So, today you're in the studio?"

"Yep, you can come and hang if you're not busy. The studio is downstairs."

"I'll try." Dani was flattered but knew she needed to keep her distance and focus on her job. "I have a phone conference with your assistant to go over some things. I'm hoping to get you organized as soon as possible."

"Hey, Dani," her best friend greeted her as she walked toward them. Melody stopped dead in her tracks when she saw Dylan. "Oh. My. God. I completely forgot to warn you about Dylan cooking in the nude." Melody hugged her.

"I didn't even notice." Dani smiled at Dylan.

"Liar." Dylan threw a hand towel at her.

"I smell bacon." Joe sat down next to Dani, grabbing a piece of bacon. He sighed. "Totally worth giving up the big house."

"I got you, bro." Dylan plated pancakes then set them on the table.

"Hell yeah." Joe grabbed a stack and went to town. "Babe, you have got to try these."

Melody joined Joe. "They smell amazing. Dani, you're going to gain an extra ten pounds by the time you leave here."

"I better step up my exercise game then." Dani snagged the last pancake before Joe grabbed it.

Joe glanced up from his plate. "You should put some clothes on. I don't think Jake and Elliot have experienced Chef Wolfgang Nude Puck, and they'll have Elijah with them."

"Right. Having a kid around kinda cramps my style." Dylan adjusted his apron like he was adjusting a designer suit.

"Don't worry," Melody said. "Dani and I will keep Elijah innocent. No need to give the poor kid night terrors."

"Hey." Dylan ran his hands down his chest seductively. "There's nothing nightmarish about this, Mellie."

The door to the cabin opened, and Tyler strode in. "What's cookin' Sweet Cheeks?"

"My man," Dylan exclaimed. "You know, the usual."

"Bacon?"

"Fuck yeah, dude!"

"Sweet." Tyler reached over Dani to grab the famous crispy pork. He looked Dani up and down as he leisurely licked the grease off his fingers. "Hey, Dani." His deep, smooth voice reminded her of velvet.

"Tyler," she greeted back.

His dark, seductive, pantie-dropping gaze met with hers. "You know, if you ever get tired of the big house, my door is always open." He winked.

Dani swallowed hard, obviously not immune to his flirting and rocker swagger sex appeal dripping from every pore. She now understood why women flocked to Tyler. "I'll keep that in mind."

A pan smacking hard against the counter broke Dani free from the rocker's spell. She looked at Dylan, who was facing the stove, cooking vigorously with a sour look on his face.

"Be careful, Dani," Joe said in between bites. "You don't know where that one has been."

Tyler flashed her a wicked grin, then hummed Johnny Cash's song, "I've Been Everywhere," as he sat at the end of the kitchen island with a plate full of food.

Dani shook her head. Never a dull moment when Gracefall was around. The bond these guys had was like family. And how lucky were they? They got to pick their family. Not that Dani was complaining about hers; she'd adapted to the Clark family's expectation, which was to be seen and not heard. It basically boiled down to staying out of trouble and keeping the Clark name squeaky clean. She was literally invisible.

"Hello," Jake called out from the front door.

"We're in the kitchen," Joe answered.

A shaggy-haired blond boy ran toward them. "Pancakes!"

"Hell—"

Dani shot Dylan a glare.

Dylan quickly corrected. "Heck yeah, little dude."

"Are you naked under that apron?" Elliot asked, confused at the sight.

"Umm." Dylan scratched his head.

Dani stepped in, grabbing a blanket from the back of the couch, and wrapping it around Dylan's waist. "Sorry about that."

Before Dani could send Dylan upstairs to get dressed, Cherry, Gracefall's tour manager, walked in with a younger blonde woman who was a striking contrast to Cherry's bright pink hair and facial piercings.

"Oh. My. God. Dylan, put on some clothes." Cherry turned to the blonde. "Are you sure you want to do this?"

The blonde stared, speechless. Dani understood; it was Dylan Grace, the rock god.

"Do what?" Joe asked.

"This is my younger sister, Tomi. She's a photographer. Against my better judgment, she's going to be photographing the band during the recording process for a behind-the-scenes promo thing that Kimmy wants done."

"Cool," Jake said as he fixed a plate of pancakes for Elijah.

"The fans will love that," Elliot added.

"Just don't make us look like a bunch of assholes," Dylan said as he gripped the blanket around his waist.

"Too late for that," Cherry teased as she looked him up and down.

"No worries," Tomi said. "You won't even know I'm here."

Dani noticed how Tyler was checking Tomi out as he walked into the kitchen and put his plate in the sink. He strolled pasted Cherry and stopped beside Tomi, giving her the same eye fucking he'd given Dani. "I highly doubt that, sweetheart." He played with a strand of Tomi's hair that had come undone from her messy bun.

Tomi's cheeks blushed, and she seemed to be just as flustered as Dani had been. Poor girl.

"No," Cherry exclaimed as she smacked Tyler's hand away from her sister's hair. "She's seventeen and off limits."

"Cherry," Tomi exclaimed, glaring at her sister.

Cherry ignored Tomi as she pushed her pink manicured fingernail against Tyler's chest. "I fucking mean it, Tyler. I'll end your man whoring days if you try something with her."

Tyler backed away with his hands in the air. "Okay, I got it." He flashed Tomi a sinful grin as he left the kitchen.

Dani looked at Dylan with a *what the hell did I just see* expression.

Dylan shrugged. "I have no idea." He gazed down at Dani and licked his lips. "Have you showered?"

Dani folded her arms across her chest. "Why?"

Dylan nodded toward the stairs leading to the bedrooms. "I'm headed up. You want to join me?"

Dani huffed. "That would be against the rules."

"Good answer." He bent down and whispered, "You passed the test."

5

*D*ylan stood under the hot spray, thinking a quick shower would ease his troubled mind. He was somewhere between I don't know, I don't care, and I don't give a fuck. The old Dylan would have been washing away an after-show hangover with a bottle of whiskey, which usually ended with a blonde, brunette, or both. He wasn't picky, nor had he any shame. With more whiskey and a line or two, he'd be ready to rock and roll all over again.

Sobriety had made him slow down and forced him to deal with the monster on his back. He wasn't sure if he was ready to deal with the chaos. To his core, he wanted to stay clean, but he was scared shitless he'd fuck up. He was one disappointment away from losing his brother and the band. Talk about pressure; Gracefall was his life. It was like he was at a pivotal crossroad, and if he chose the wrong path, it'd be the slippery slope leading to his downfall.

Add a sexy-as-sin Dani to the picture, and he was totally fucked.

Seeing her this morning with her long black hair tossed back in a ponytail, her lips painted red, the same shade she always wore, and the way her jeans hugged her firm ass made him beg for mercy. She had no clue what her sultry blue eyes did to him. Even though in the past he'd been blitzed out of his mind, he'd never forget the way they'd fucked. Being in Dani's bed with his cock buried deep inside her was like being reborn. It was like floating up to heaven and giving God a high five, thanking Him for an amazing woman.

She was the one chick who really understood him. He could talk to her about all kinds of shit. Movies, life on the road, and even his ex if you could believe it. They had a connection like nothing he'd had before, and that made him scared...and horny.

Reminiscing about Dani made him want to grab his cock and indulge in the fantasy, but he wouldn't do it. Maybe the old Dylan would have reached down to give himself the ole razzle-dazzle. Hell, the old Dylan would have had her on the kitchen table this morning, fucking her into oblivion.

Dylan fell forward, resting his hands on the tiled shower wall, and sighed. He didn't know how to feel about Dani, except there was something about her that lit up a room. What he did know was when she was around, his world was a little bit sweeter, which was why nothing could ever happen between them.

That thought alone left a hole in his heart. "Fuck!"

Dylan didn't want to be another rock star cliché, but he wasn't going to lie to himself either. He was hardwired to self-destruct, and it was only a matter of time before the fuse was lit. And for that reason alone, Dani would stay off limits. He wouldn't bring her into his madness; Dani deserved better.

Dylan needed to focus on the next album. He was already feeling twitchy about recording sober. His previous recording routine included a bottle of bourbon and a few lines of coke before he could belt out some lyrics. Somewhere down the line, he became tolerant of the drugs and needed more to keep balanced. So yeah, he couldn't remember a time in the studio or on stage when he wasn't completely blitzed.

Could he still perform at the same level he'd been performing under the influence? Had he lost his edge?

The songwriting was still there, if not better. That was Dylan's escape, his therapy. Growing up poor with a mother who was addicted to drugs and beaten by her boyfriends, he had a lot of shit to filter through. Expressing his abuse through song was a lot easier than talking about it. Even though Melody's father had taken him and Joe in, the damage had already been done. He kept the nightmare a secret. Not even his brother knew the extent of the abuse, and quite frankly, neither did he when drunk and high.

Fuck, clarity was a bitch.

Still confused and now more anxious, Dylan shut off the shower and dried himself. He padded across the hardwood floor to his walk-in closet. He hadn't taken the time to hang his clothes; he'd kept them in the suitcase like he'd always done, even as a kid. Keeping his bags packed gave him the security that he could bolt at any time. However, as a child, he never had the guts to follow through. He couldn't leave big bro.

Old habits were hard to break.

Dylan pulled out a pair of ripped jeans, a black T-shirt, and a gray hoodie. With a quick once-over in the mirror, he zipped up his cotton-blend jacket, grabbed the notebook of songs he had been working on, and headed downstairs. He'd hoped he might see Dani before going into the studio, but she wasn't there. In fact, no one was downstairs, which meant the band was waiting on him.

Outside the studio door, Dylan paced, chewing on the cuticle on his thumbnail, not able to will himself to go inside. He couldn't do this; he wasn't ready.

"Hey, Dylan," Jake greeted him with obvious concern on his face. "Everything okay?"

"Yeah." Dylan paused. "I need a minute to collect my thoughts."

"Should I call Dani?"

Why would he call Dani? It wasn't like she'd bring him a bottle of whiskey to calm his nerves.

"I can text Elliot." Jake pulled out his cell.

No, he didn't need Elliot the Sponsor; he needed Elliot the Kickass Guitarist. "Jake, you need to cool your shit. I'm fine," he lied.

"Right. Sorry, dude. It must feel weird, you know, being sober."

"I'm good." He faked a smile.

"Good." Jake clasped his shoulder, giving some comfort. "Everyone is inside."

Knowing Jake had his back meant a lot. He'd hit it off right from the start with the new lead guitarist. Dylan would have been six feet under if it wasn't for Jake and Elliot, rockin' it with the devil himself. "Let's do this."

Dylan walked behind Jake into a nicely sized sitting area with cream leather couches, a rustic coffee table that sat between the sofas, and a wet bar that took up a corner of the room. Overhead, a round chandelier with lights that resembled candles hung by black chains, casting a warm glow over the space.

"Everyone is in here," Jake said and directed Dylan

through a stone-arched doorway that led into an enormous studio.

Dylan couldn't believe his eyes. There were two isolation booths, one set up for vocals and one for drums on opposite sides of the room. In all its polished, aged-wood glory, a grand piano stood off to the side on a stage equipped with microphone stands, amps, and another drum set where Joe was sitting on the throne conversing with Tyler. Standing next to the piano, Elliot, the Queen of Shred, was warming up her signature Ibanez guitar. The band was ready, but was he?

In the middle of the far wall between the isolation booths, Alex, who was producing Gracefall's album, and their sound engineer sat behind a plexiglass wall inside the control room like the Great Oz, ready to make magic.

"You're late." Joe scoffed behind his drum kit. Silence filled the room.

"Sorry." Dylan shrugged. "Guess I lost track of time."

"Maybe Dani can help you with managing your time better."

Dylan didn't understand why his brother was being a dick. He was only fifteen minutes late. He ignored the remark and opened up his notebook. "I've been working on a few songs." Dylan grabbed an acoustic guitar that had been hanging on the wall. He wasn't the best at playing, but he'd make it work to introduce the songs.

"Jake and I have it covered," Joe said.

Confusion washed over Dylan. What the fuck was going on? "Joe, we write the songs together. It's always been that way."

"I know, but Jake has some excellent stuff."

"What about what I have written?"

"We're going to start with the song Jake wrote, then we'll see how it goes."

"What the fuck? I get no say-so over the writing? Why?"

"Dylan, it's just one song," Tyler added. "It's no big deal."

Dylan felt as if he was going to explode. "No big deal?"

"Listen, why don't we see what Dylan has written," Jake said as he adjusted his guitar strap.

"No. Fuck you, Jake," Dylan growled.

"Dylan, calm down." Elliot began to walk over to him, but he held up his hand, stopping her.

"I like you, Elliot, so stay out of it." Dylan watched her retreat a step. He focused on his brother. "This is my band too. If you got something personal against me, let's settle it outside of the band. Don't bring our shit in here."

Joe got up and walked toward him. His steel-gray eyes pinned him with so much hatred. "You gave up your rights to the band when you pulled that shit at my engagement party. You've been too messed up to care about anyone but yourself and how Ash fucked you over."

"Oh, that's rich." Dylan laid the guitar down before he ended up swinging the damn thing into the drum set. "You bring up the past. I went to rehab just like you told me. I've accepted your bullshit idea of having a life coach and agreed to no sex. Am I ever going to be forgiven?"

Joe stepped closer, and they were now eye to eye with tempers flaring. "I told you I'd do whatever it takes to keep Gracefall together, and if that means keeping you on a short leash, I'll do it."

Dylan moved even closer, bumping Joe's chest with his. "I'm not a fucking dog that takes orders from its handler."

Joe worked his jaw, twitching and clenching it. He cracked his neck, ready for a fight. If this was what Joe wanted, Dylan would give it to him.

Dylan pushed Joe's chest. "Let's do this."

"Okay." Tyler stepped in and grabbed Dylan's arm. "Let's take five and cool off."

"Fuck you, dude." Dylan yanked his arm away. "You're okay with this?"

"I'm okay with lessening the stress on you while you recover."

Dylan stepped back and laughed. "They got to you too."

Dylan glared at Joe. His brother stared at him with stone coldness. He didn't understand where the hostility was coming from. There was something else going on, but Dylan couldn't put his finger on it. Instead of pushing further, Dylan dropped it and headed toward the door.

"Bro." Tyler followed him. "Where are you going?"

"It's obvious I'm not needed." Dylan turned around, giving them the middle finger, one on each hand. "I'm out."

6

*T*he next morning Dani was up early, dressed in her black yoga pants and gray crop top sweatshirt in preparation for Dylan's meditation session. She'd talked herself out of going to the studio last night and instead immersed herself in her work. After a phone conference with Dylan's assistant, Dani had a lot more work than she'd thought. She had to review his social media accounts, his schedule, and put together a personal and financial growth plan, all by herself. And it wasn't like she was getting much help from Dylan.

As Dani laid down her yoga mat in front of the fireplace in the living room, her mind still spun with images posted on Dylan's social media sites. Pics of Gracefall shows from all over the world, selfies with fans, and one she wished she hadn't come across of the lead singer from *Blushing Alice*, Ashley Monroe, and him backstage at a concert.

Dylan had talked a lot about Ash, to the point Dani felt like she knew her, though they never had met. Even so, she knew Ash's favorite breakfast items, eggs over easy and toast, but Dani knew very little about her relationship with Dylan. Whatever happened had left Dylan gutted. It was no surprise why he'd fallen for Ash. She was beautiful with badass vocal talent. She had long, red hair; chestnut, doe-like eyes; and her skin was flawless. Her lively smile was infectious. Dani had even caught herself smiling back at the photographs because, of course, she'd been stalking the redhead's social media accounts. As if her beauty hadn't been enough, she had talent, which took her to the next level of badassery. But beyond all of that, she had Dylan's heart, and Dani couldn't compete with that.

But Dani couldn't blame her or any other one of his groupies. She'd known what she was getting into. She'd been just another girl in another city. It was her fault she'd let him get into her heart.

Dani walked over to the wall of windows that overlooked the mountain views. The sky was gray, just like her mood had turned. Thinking of what she'd meant to Dylan throughout the past couple of years left her heartbroken and depressed. Their friendship had been purely sexual. It wasn't his fault; she'd allowed it to happen. She'd known she couldn't hold on to something that wasn't hers to keep. Ash had reminded her of that. That thought alone sent a chill over her body. Dani rubbed her arms, but the coldness was still there.

"I think it's going to snow today." Dani turned around as Dylan walked toward her in all his rock and roll swagger wearing nothing but a pair of ripped jeans and holding a leather-bound notebook. Speechless, she took in the rock star's muscular body. A black and gray raven with its wings stretched out covered his upper chest. As he scratched his bearded chin, her attention was drawn to his lean arms, which were also covered in tattoos. The man's body was a work of art.

Dani cleared her throat. "Yeah, at least five inches."

"That's enough to build a snowman."

"I wouldn't know. This is my first snow."

"Really?"

"Why would that surprise you? I live in LA."

"Right. I just thought with famous parents that you might have traveled a lot. You know, like ski vacations and shit."

Dani shook her head. "No, I barely saw my parents. They were busy on set most of the time." Yep, Mr. and Mrs. Daytime Soap Opera Star were Hollywood's dream team. Not only were they married in the real world, they were married on the show, and everyone loved them. Dani just wished her parents would bring that kind of love home to her—at least a fraction of it.

She guessed in a way they had to some degree. Throughout her life she'd never gone without. Dani had gone to the top schools, worn designer clothes, had been gifted a brand-new BMW sportscar for her sixteenth birthday. Yeah, she'd grown up in fame, but she had stayed grounded thanks to her Aunt Meg, her mom's sister. Meg was the mother she yearned for.

So yeah, it was unfair to ask more of her parents than they were capable of giving.

"When we did go on vacation, we went to the beach." Dani folded her arms. She didn't want to recall the numerous beach vacations she'd spent with Meg wishing her parents were there. "How about you?"

Dylan chuckled. "If you call driving out to the liquor store in the middle of the night a vacation, then I took a lot of them."

"But, hey, look at you now. You've traveled the world. I can't imagine all the places you've seen."

"I mean, Paris was kickass from what I remember." Dylan cracked a half smile, which made her laugh.

Dani walked over to the yoga mat. "I was going to set up on the deck. The view out there is amazing, but it's too cold for this LA girl."

"Wimp," Dylan teased.

Dani sat down on the mat, crossing her legs. She gazed up at Dylan and patted the floor next to her.

Dylan scratched his bearded chin. "We're really doing this, huh?"

Dani straightened her spine, tilted her head back, and closed her eyes. The heat from the fireplace warmed her comfortably. "Yep."

Suddenly, Dani felt the weight of Dylan's head lying in her lap. She looked down at him. Their gazes met. "What are you doing?"

"I'm meditating." He squirmed, making himself comfortable.

"In my lap?"

"It's where I feel the most comfortable." He closed his eyes, and Dani didn't argue. At least he was trying.

She started the meditation app on her phone, then set it down next to them. "So, just listen and do what is instructed. Clear your mind by taking in deep breaths then letting them out." Dani illustrated the breathing technique a couple times before she noticed Dylan not doing it. "Why aren't you breathing?"

"You know, you have perfect tits?"

Dani's body deflated. She opened her eyes to find Dylan staring at her breasts. "How is this supposed to work if you're not taking it seriously?"

"I can't help it. Your tits are basically in my face. Besides, the chick's voice on the app is annoying. No one ever sounds that peaceful. I'm not buying it."

Dani huffed. "You need to focus."

"You need to let me focus on your tits. That's all the meditation I need." He flashed her a wicked, crooked smile. That smile alone was the reason the guy got away with murder.

Dani closed her eyes, returning to the woman's voice on the app. God, he was right; the chick was annoying. "In with the good air and out with the bad."

A few minutes passed, and now Dani was having a hard time focusing. The scent of his woodsy cologne, which blended with his natural clean male scent perfectly, was driving her hormones into overdrive. Maybe breathing wasn't such a good idea. "So, how did things go in the studio last night?"

"I thought we were meditating."

Dani looked down at him. His eyes were closed, and he looked so peaceful. She resisted the urge to run her fingertips through his short blond hair. "I know, but I was wondering how it went. I bet it felt good to be creating music again."

"Yeah, not so much." Dylan opened his eyes, and she saw that something was wrong.

"What happened?" She hoped he would talk about whatever happened in the studio. With Dylan, she didn't know what to expect. Some things were off-limits, and she was still learning the boundaries. They were complete opposites. She was an open book and would talk about anything, while Dylan was closed off. However, in the past, Dani had been able to ease his troubles. She knew when he needed her, regardless of if

Dylan knew it or not. Also, it helped that she was a good listener.

"Since the beginning of Gracefall, Joe and I wrote all the songs. I did most of the writing. It's like therapy. Yesterday, Joe took that away from me."

Dani heard the anger in his voice as he sat up. "I came in with new material, and he didn't even want to see it. Instead, everyone agreed to have Jake write the songs. They didn't even ask me. If Mox was still alive, this shit wouldn't be going down."

The band had been at the height of their career when Moxley Sims died in a tragic bus accident. It was a huge blow to the band. No one in the band had dealt with Mox's death fully. Sex, drugs, and denial were the Band-Aids covering a gaping wound on the soul of Gracefall. When Dylan had told her about the late guitarist's death and how Gracefall was going back on the road a week after his funeral, she had been concerned. Now, she hated that she had been right. Hiding behind all of the rock and roll indulgencies, Mox's death was still haunting the band.

"I'm sure there's a reason why."

"Sure there was. They're concerned about my stress level," Dylan mocked. "So, I'm just supposed to show up and sing someone else's songs? Fuck that. Do I look stressed out?"

Dani pursed her lips together as she thought about her next words carefully. He did look on edge. "I wouldn't say stressed. Look, could the band be concerned about you relapsing? Maybe that's why they want to help lower your stress level until you're one hundred percent."

"I don't know." Frustrated, Dylan scrubbed his face. "It feels like no matter what I do, it's never good enough for Joe.

You know the a-hole only visited me once when I was in rehab?"

"Really? I didn't know."

"Yep, we got into a huge fight, which led to me spending the holidays alone. Oh, I did get the Christmas cookies you sent. Thank you."

"You're welcome. I can't believe that you spent Christmas alone. I tried to see you, but they said that you weren't accepting visitors. I thought you were spending the holidays with your family."

Dylan shook his head. "No, I requested no visitors the rest of the time I was in rehab. I couldn't deal with Joe and his self-righteousness."

Dani didn't know what to think. No one should spend the holidays alone. "I wish I had known what was going on. I'm surprised Melody didn't say anything."

"I don't think Joe told her." Dylan pinned her with his blue-gray stare that went straight to her heart. "Dani, us Grace brothers are all kinds of fucked up."

His confession would have brought her to her knees if she wasn't sitting. "Everyone is redeemable."

"Even a serial killer?"

Dani shot him a stunned look.

"Christ, Dani, I'm not a serial killer."

"Well, I was talking about redeeming yourself, not forgiveness. I think you need to talk to Joe and tell him how you feel."

Dylan sat quietly for a moment, pondering. "You know your positivity is annoying?" he teased.

Dani smiled. "I know, but it's my job to annoy you and keep you out of trouble."

"You're doing a good job."

Dani shrugged.

Their eyes met, and for a moment the world stood still. Looking into Dylan's gaze, she saw someone struggling to find peace, and it broke her heart. Dylan was a good man; he was just a little lost.

Dylan cleared his throat as he broke their moment. "If Mox were here, he'd have supported me. He was the backbone of the band. Without him..." Dylan exhaled and scrubbed his hand through his hair.

Reading Dylan's expression, Dani saw that he wasn't comfortable talking about Mox, so she let it go. "Mox was a special guy and is dearly missed. But I know how much Gracefall meant to him, and he wouldn't want anything to jeopardize its success. I also think he'd be proud of you."

Dylan locked eyes with her. "Really? You think he'd be proud of me?"

Dani smiled. "I do. Getting clean is a huge accomplishment. Addiction is giving up everything for one thing. Recovery is giving up one thing for everything. You chose recovery. That's huge."

Dylan was silent, but by the look on his face, his brain was in overdrive.

After a brief moment, Dylan sat up and spoke. "And that, my friends, was a deep thought by Dani Clark."

Deflated in all hopes she had gotten through to him, Dani shook her head. There was no getting through. Just when she thought they were making progress, Dylan deflected to something else.

"I should probably try to go to work today." Dylan stood and offered his hand to help her up.

"Yeah, I think you should." Dani rose to her feet. "I have to run into town for a couple of things. I'll have my cell on me if you need me for anything."

Dylan's brow rose. "Anything?"

For a split second, his sexual innuendo had Dani's girly parts ready for a long-overdue reunion with Dylan's cock. What that man's lips and tongue did to her body; she didn't know if she had the strength to deny him.

"Anything but sex."

It was a terrible idea. Dani bent down to roll up her mat when she felt Dylan staring at her ass. She stood up, tucking the yoga mat under her arm. Desire from his lustful gaze caused a rush of heat to blaze through her body. Her inner good girl warred with her naughty girl thoughts. All she had to do was make the first move, and they'd be right back to their old habits.

"Dani, I have been very patient with you."

What was he talking about?

"But if you keep breaking rule number three, we're going to have a problem."

Puzzled, she tried to recall the rules. Maybe she should have written them down. "I don't understand."

"Don't look at me like you want to fuck me."

"I'm not. You're the one that keeps ogling my boobs and butt."

Dylan laughed.

"What?"

"You look at me like you're going to eat me alive, but you can't even say tits and ass."

"First of all, you're reading into things."

"Am I?"

"Yes, you are. I'm not interested in sleeping with you. It's strictly business between you and me. Besides, I know what you're trying to do."

"Okay, Dr. Cupcake." He folded his arms. "What am I doing?"

"You're trying to get rid of me, and it's not working."

"Huh." He stared at her intently. That same go-weak-in-the-knees gaze. "I rest my case." He turned toward the stairs to leave.

"What?" She threw her arms up. "I didn't do anything."

He continued downstairs with a cocky smirk on his face. Dani didn't know if it was his arrogance, the smirk, or the rocker attitude that irritated her the most.

Frustrated, she strode to the staircase railing and yelled, "You are impossible, Dylan Grace!"

~

*H*ours later, Dani stood in the checkout line at the local general store, waiting to buy her red heart-shaped string lights. With Valentine's Day right around the corner, the store looked as if Cupid threw up all over the place.

She'd felt horrible about Dylan spending the holidays alone and wanted to plan a small belated Christmas for him to brighten his mood. Even though right now, all she wanted to do was knock him on his butt. She wasn't letting him get away with his little stunt. He was pushing her away, and now she had to push back harder. Dylan might think of her as Miss Goody Two-shoes, but he hadn't seen her stubborn side.

After searching the cabin for a fake Christmas tree and coming up empty-handed, Dani had driven into town in search of one. To her disappointment, the only store close by was a general store. A winter snowstorm was forecast by nightfall, so she didn't have much time to waste. With Christmas long gone, she thought maybe she'd get lucky and find a small fake tree in the clearance section. No such luck. Looks like she would have to cut one down herself.

Dani paid for the lights, a couple bags of Dylan's favorite candy, and an axe she'd found in the hardware section. As she eyed the small blade on the handle, she dismissed the plan of having a grand Christmas tree and accepted the fact a Christmas twig would have to do.

A blast of cold air hit Dani as she opened the door and walked to her car. The sky was darker, and snow flurries were falling fast, leaving a white dusting on the ground. She'd never driven in the snow before. She prayed she'd make it up the mountain safely. But first, she needed warmth.

Tossing the bags in the backseat, Dani slid into the car and started it. She cranked the heat as she rubbed her hands on her thighs for warmth. Yep, she couldn't wait to go back home and soak in the California sunshine.

Thirty minutes into her drive back to the cabin, Dani was still treeless. With forest all around her, she would have thought she'd see a sign on the side of the road for a nursery. Then again, who would be open with a snowstorm coming? Who would be out in the snow looking for a tree? A stubborn woman who wasn't going to let a little weather stop her from getting the perfect Christmas tree, that's who.

Dani was running out of real estate and time; Pine Mountain was ahead. Not knowing what else to do, she pulled over and parked. A cold breeze nipped at her face as she stepped out of the car holding the small axe. The forest terrain was flat, and there were evergreen trees as far as her eyes could see. The perfect tree had to be in there somewhere.

Dani pulled her gray wool beanie down to cover her ears

and snuggled deeper into her coat as she walked toward the tree line. Her boots crunched through the snow, leaving a trail behind her. It was a good thing; she didn't want to get lost in the forest. The only survival skill she had from the city was navigating through traffic on the freeway.

She didn't know how long she'd been on the hunt before she finally found a small spruce her tiny axe could handle. She shook the snow off the sapling and sized it up, deciding which direction she was going to start chopping. Dani had no clue. She'd never pulled a weed in her life, let alone a tree. Growing up, they'd had landscapers and hired professional decorators to spread Christmas cheer throughout the estate.

The wind blew, and another chill consumed her body. She was pretty sure she couldn't feel her toes. Dani swung her axe into the trunk of the spruce. After a few hits, the blade hadn't made a dent. *Crap!*

Out of breath, Dani stood up and gazed at the tree. "This is stupid." For a little tree, the trunk was strong as steel. She wiped the sweat from her brow then readied herself to take another swing.

"Miss, do you have a permit?"

Dani turned around to find a huge, muscular man wearing an army green jacket. His muscles strained against his clothing, making him look like the Hulk was about to rip through. She'd read the tall tales of Paul Bunyan but had never met the lumberjack until now.

"Do you have a permit?" The man's voice sounded agitated.

Dani finally came to. "No, I didn't know I needed one."

"Ma'am, this is a national park. You need a permit for cutting down trees." He eyed the axe in her hand. "That is what you're doing, yes?"

Heat rose to her cheeks as embarrassment flooded over her. "I'm not from around here." Crap, what was she thinking? Hello, stranger danger. "I should go. My friend is waiting for me in the car."

"You mean the unoccupied red sports car parked on the side of the road?"

Dani froze. This was it. There was no way she'd be able to fight off the hulking lumberjack. She was going to be murdered. She gripped her axe.

"Relax. My name is Ben, and I'm a park ranger for the Pine Mountain National Park." He flashed his badge.

She exhaled. This was definitely better than getting murdered; however, she'd never had a run-in with the law, not even a speeding ticket. "Hi Ben, I'm Dani. I didn't know this was a national park."

"What are you doing to this poor tree?" Ben bent down and examined her chopping skills.

"I'm trying to cheer up a friend."

"You know they have florists for that," he teased.

"I know." She laughed. "My friend spent Christmas alone, so I thought bringing home a tree to decorate would bring cheer."

Ben stood, brushing the snow from his pants. "That's kind of you. Everyone should have a friend like you."

Dani blushed. Why was she blushing? Maybe it was Ben's warm, chestnut-brown eyes checking her out. It had been a while since she'd been hit on, and it was nice.

"So, listen, I can help you out. You can have the sapling, and I'll forget what I saw here today if you agree to go out on a date with me. That's if you're single."

"I am single."

"So…"

Dani thought about it. Maybe this was exactly what she

needed to get Dylan off her mind. Ben was handsome in a woodsy kind of way, and he seemed nice. And God, that white, toothy smile was enough to bring any woman to her knees. "Yeah, I'll go on a date with you."

"Yeah?"

Dani nodded. "I mean, I'm sure there's a hefty fine for cutting down a tree in a national park."

"Oh, you better believe it. Starting at eight-hundred dollars." Ben began bending the tree back and forth, loosening the root ball.

"Well, consider me lucky." They shared a smile.

In no time, Ben had the small spruce tied to the hood of Dani's rental.

"That should do it," Ben said as he took off his sap-covered gloves. He reached into the inside pocket of his jacket and pulled out a card. "Here's my number." He handed it to Dani.

She checked her pockets. "I don't have anything to write on. Do you have your cell on you?"

Ben pulled out his phone and brought up his contact list. "You can add it here."

Dani added her number then handed his cell back.

They stood for a moment in awkward silence. Well, it felt awkward to Dani. "The snow is picking up. You should get home before the roads are undrivable," Ben said.

"Yeah, you're probably right." She grinned. "Thank you for helping me out."

Ben nodded. "It was nice meeting you, Dani." He opened her car door. "Drive safe, and I'll see you soon."

Dani got in the car, and he shut the door behind her. Gosh, he was even a gentleman. Something had to be wrong with him. Why was a nice guy like Ben still single? Maybe he had terrible table manners. No one likes a guy who chews with his mouth open. That had to be it.

Dani turned the engine over. She waved goodbye to Ben before she pulled onto the road. Dani exhaled, thankful to be heading back to the cabin. Now she had to come up with a plan to get the tree in the house without Dylan knowing.

7

*D*ylan sat behind the control panel in the studio after the band had left for the night. He'd persuaded Alex, Gracefall's producer, to stay longer and help iron out some kinks to a song the band had recorded. Dylan had swallowed his pride and attempted to sing the song, but it was shit.

He'd been in the studio all day, trying not to lose his head. The song Jake had written was going nowhere. The melody was off the way Jakey boy had written it. Dylan had pleaded his case, but of course, he was accused of being difficult. No, he knew when he heard shit, and this was pure shit. The guitar riff was off, and the beat was off. They'd wasted a whole day of recording because the band couldn't come together.

If he couldn't have control over writing the song, he would have control over the sound. Dylan listened to the playback. Jake's guitar solo started, and Dylan cringed. "Alex, let's increase Tyler's bass right here and see how it sounds." He wasn't sure if it was the riff or the fact he was still pissed at Jake and wanted to stick it to him. Jake needed to know his place. Whichever it was, Jake's guitar riff was going to be muffled. Dylan knew that it was best to have the band here to make these decisions, but no one was getting along, and he didn't want to waste time. So, here he was, fixing a hot mess.

Dylan leaned back in the chair, listening to the solo with more bass punch. "Fuck yeah, dude!" He bounced his head to the beat. "That's a winner."

Alex nodded. "For sure. Should we call the guys back in?"

"Nah, it can wait until tomorrow. I think they'll like it."

"Okay, then that's a wrap," Alex said. "I need food."

"Go ahead. I'll shut down."

As Alex left, Dylan played back the track, tweaking his vocals, and boom, the song was perfect.

Dylan shut everything down and headed upstairs. He made his way through the hallway to the living room. All the lights were off except for a red glow near the fireplace. He walked over to examine what was going on. A small spruce tree decorated in heart-shaped red lights sat in front of the window. The snow falling behind the tree reminded him of Christmas.

"Hey."

He turned around and saw Dani wearing an apron with flour on her nose.

"Merry Christmas!" She beamed and motioned to the tree.

Dylan was confused. "It's February. Shouldn't we be celebrating Valentine's Day?"

"No." Dani walked toward him. "We're celebrating Christmas." She stood next to him, gazing at the tree. "What do you think?"

Dylan didn't know what to think. "You did this for me?"

"Of course. No one should ever spend Christmas alone. So, tonight we're watching Christmas movies and eating Christmas cookies."

"You made cookies?"

"I did." She beamed, and it was cutest thing he'd ever seen.

No one had ever done something this thoughtful for him. Ever. Christmas was just another day. There had never been a tree in his house growing up, let alone gifts under it. Not until Melody's dad had taken him and Joe in. The Sterling's always had a giant Christmas tree and an even bigger Christmas family dinner, to which he and Joe were always invited. However, he'd felt like an outsider looking in, and it had only made him yearn for a family like Mel's.

"Is everything okay?" Dani looked as if she'd done something wrong, which was the last thing he wanted her to feel.

Dylan smiled as he wiped the smudge of flour from her nose. "It's perfect." But what he wanted to say was *"You are perfect."*

His hands moved to frame her face. He stared deep into her vibrant blue eyes. For the first time, he noticed how beautiful they were. Sky blue. Sobriety was definitely worth it.

His gaze moved to her mouth. Full, pink, kissable lips tested his resolve. Especially now, as she nervously bit her bottom lip like she was waiting for him to make the first move. He wanted to kiss her. Fuck, he did. How much sweeter would she taste now that he was sober?

He wasn't going to find out. Not with Dani. She deserved better.

Dylan was about to step away when he felt her body shudder. "Dani, you're shivering."

~

*Y*eah, Dani was shivering. Dylan kinda did that to her every damn time their bodies collided. He made her want to throw her good sense aside and drown in sin. And what a beautiful sin he was. Worst of all, he made her want to fall in love.

Dani thought after months of being apart and all he'd been through that whatever they'd had was dead, but it obviously wasn't. They still had some kind of crazy chemistry.

Dani took a step back, breaking free from his smoldering gaze. "Is it cold in here?" She rubbed her arms.

Dylan flashed her a lopsided smile that said he didn't believe her. "Thank you for tonight, Dani. I really needed a friend."

There was that feeling again. The feeling of Dani's insides melting, her knees going weak, and her heart flip-flopping like a fish out of water. She inhaled deeply, calming her raging hormones. "Was it that bad?"

Dylan scrubbed his hair. "Yeah, the whole recording session was shit. I don't know how much more can go down before the band explodes."

"Have you talked to Joe?"

Dylan shook his head. "It's impossible to talk to him."

"Maybe actions speak louder than words with him. You need to show him how you're feeling."

"What is that supposed to mean? I feel like kicking his ass."

"No. No need to get violent. Is there a place you can take Joe that holds sentimental value to you both where you guys could talk?"

"Dani, I grew up in a trailer park. My mom is addicted to drugs. There are no warm fuzzies here."

"I just thought—"

"Listen, I understand what you're saying, but I really don't want to talk about it tonight. I just want to sit on the couch and eat cookies with a friend. What say you?"

The mention of friends made her smile. She liked that. "Okay, I'll go get the cookies and milk. You find a movie." Dani started toward the kitchen then paused, remembering that it was probably not a good idea to give Dylan that much freedom. "No porn."

"Aw, come on, Dani, you're no fun."

Dani returned shortly with a plate of frosted sugar cookies in Christmas shapes and two glasses of milk. She set everything down on the coffee table then sat down on the couch next to Dylan. She handed him a glass and snowflake cookie. "I figured these were appropriate since it's snowing outside."

"Did you decorate all these cookies?"

"I tried." She had, but her decorating skills were limited.

"They look amazing."

"You don't have to be nice, Dylan. The snowflakes are supposed to be light blue, not purple." She laughed as she handed him a glass of milk. "Cheers." She held up her glass, and Dylan followed.

"To friendship."

"To friendship," Dani agreed. "So, what are we watching?" She got comfortable, snuggling into the couch, sitting with her legs curled up against her.

Dylan set his glass down, then laid down on the couch with his head on Dani's lap. "*It's a Wonderful Life.*"

Dani was surprised. "Good choice. I would have thought you'd pick *Die Hard.*"

"That's next."

Dani smiled. She couldn't think of a more perfect night. Flames were flickering and crackling in the fireplace, the snow was steadily coming down outside, her belly was full of cookies, and Dylan Grace was using her as a pillow.

"This is the most wholesome thing I've ever done," Dylan said, pulling Dani out of her daydream musings.

"Wholesome isn't so bad, is it?"

"Can I be honest?"

"Sure."

"I'd rather be fucking you."

She felt his grip tighten around her leg. The heat from his touch shot a buzz racing through her veins. God, it would be so easy to fall back into old habits. She took in a deep breath, trying not to think about Dylan's hot, tattooed body lying on top of her or how his touch turned her on. No, she wasn't going there.

"I do appreciate you being honest, but that won't be happening."

"I know, cupcake. It's really a shame to let all this sexual tension go to waste."

"Dylan, just watch the movie."

"I still get you hot and bothered."

"You know nothing."

"We'll see."

Dani rolled her eyes. His arrogance was irritating. Just because he was a rock star didn't mean he got everything he wanted.

8

*D*ylan was up early the next morning to shower and head down to the studio to get started on a long and grueling day. It should have sent him straight into a bad mood, but it didn't. He felt refreshed. Dylan couldn't remember the last time he'd gotten a peaceful night's sleep. Shit, he'd even hummed in the shower. What the fuck was going on? Dani's optimistic vibe and positivity must have been rubbing off on him.

They'd spent most of the night together watching Christmas movies until she had fallen asleep. He'd picked her up and tucked her into bed. But before he left, he had stayed and watched her sleep. Yeah, creepy, but there was something so peaceful about her that he couldn't bring himself to leave. He'd stroked her long black hair from her face as he studied her smooth, soft features, her high cheekbones, and full, kissable lips.

She was gorgeous and intelligent, and life was easier when she was around. Why was she hanging out with a fucked-up rock star?

Dylan shook free from that thought; nothing was

breaking his stride today. He was high on life. Or high on the feeling that he'd see Dani this morning in the studio.

He headed downstairs to the studio. Dani, Mel, and Elliot were hanging out on the couch when he walked in.

"Ladies," he greeted them with a smile.

"You seem chipper this morning," Elliot said as she sipped her coffee.

Dylan shoved his hands in the front pockets of his jeans. "It's all good." His eyes went straight to Dani. God, she looked hot when her cheeks blushed.

"Hey, asshole!" Jake shouted from the other room as he strode toward him. "What the fuck is your problem?"

Confusion washed over Dylan. "I don't know what you're talking about."

Elliot held onto Jake's arm, stopping him from coming closer. "Jake, what's going on?"

"Dylan fucked with the song we recorded yesterday after we all left."

At that moment, Joe and Tyler rushed in and screeched to a halt after seeing Jake and Dylan standing toe-to-toe.

"I'm sure it was for the better," Elliot reassured.

"Fuck yeah, it was." Dylan popped his neck from side to side as he glared at Jake. "You're welcome."

"You removed my guitar track." Jake shoved Dylan.

Dylan stumbled back. "What the fuck, dude?"

"Enough." Joe stepped between the egos. "To be honest, Jake, the song sounds better."

Wait, what? Joe was on his side?

"You're just saying that because he's your brother." Jake stood down after Joe gave him an *oh, you just didn't go there* scowl.

"Joe's right," Tyler said.

"You would say that." Jake pointed at Tyler. "It's your bass track that everyone hears."

"Look," Dylan started. "Your guitar track is still there. It's just dialed down."

"Fuck you, Dylan. You know what your problem is?"

Dylan snickered and folded his arms. "No, but please enlighten me. Therapy's getting too expensive."

"It kills you not to be in control. You're scared that if you allow someone else in the band to contribute, you'll be out of a job."

Jake hit a nerve, a deep one. Dylan balled his fists, cracking his knuckles. He took in a deep breath. "Jake, this is my band. I sing the songs. Therefore, I have the last word. It's how Gracefall rolls. Don't take it personal." It took all of Dylan's resolve not to haul off and knock Jake out.

"I bet you never treated Moxley this way."

Like a needle sliding across a record, the room came to a halt. All eyes were on Jake.

Dylan shoved past Joe and got into Jake's face. "You'll never be Mox. Not even close."

Jake's jaw flexed as he leaned back. Then he threw his head forward, headbutting Dylan. The frontman stumbled back, and before he could get his bearings straight, Jake punched him in the face. Blood poured from his nose.

"Motherfucker, you better not have broken my nose." Like a wild animal, Dylan charged Jake, knocking him on his ass.

"Let it go!" Joe yelled.

The taste of blood flooded Dylan's mouth. He spat on the floor next to Jake. Elliot was bent down next to Jake, glaring up at him. He turned his attention to Dani, who looked like she was in shock.

Dylan wiped his nose with the back of his hand. "Are we

done?" He looked at Joe, then to Tyler, then back to Jake. No one said a word. "Thought so." Dylan turned and strode out of the studio.

~

*T*he sun was setting, and Dani paced in her bedroom. Since Jake and Dylan's fight, she'd kept herself busy, giving Dylan time to cool off. He'd been in his bedroom all day blaring metal music. It gave her some comfort that he couldn't leave the cabin because they were still snowed in on the mountain. Jake bringing up Mox was a low blow that had hit Dylan hard. She'd seen the torment on his face. Dylan was ninety-plus days sober and vulnerable. With all the trouble brewing in the band, she feared something like this would send him over the edge.

It was killing Dani knowing he was all alone dealing with his demons. Whether he knew it or not, he needed her, and she needed to know he was okay. Dani looked at the clock sitting on the dresser. Five o'clock. She'd given him enough time.

Dani strode out of her bedroom, her bare feet moving across the soft oriental rug leading her down the hall. Dylan's room wasn't far, yet it felt like a mile away. She knocked on the door, hoping he'd hear her over the loud music. "Dylan, it's me, Dani."

"Go away!" His voice was low and deep, and it scared her. He didn't sound good.

"I can't do that."

"You're not coming in, Dani."

"You can either let me in civilly, or I'll get Mac to knock down the door. Your choice."

The music stopped. Dani stood outside the door,

patiently waiting. He wasn't going anywhere, and she wasn't leaving.

The door opened slowly. Dylan, only wearing a pair of ripped jeans, stood in the doorframe. "Damn, Dani, you don't have to sound like the Big Bad Wolf."

"Very funny." Dani pushed her way inside.

As soon as she walked in, his spicy, woodsy cologne assaulted her senses, turning on her naughty thoughts. God, he smelled good. His bedroom layout was like hers; a stone-faced fireplace and a wall of windows overlooked the snow-capped mountains. She didn't trust herself to look at the oversized bed filled with decorative cabin-chic pillows and blankets. Nope, she wasn't looking.

Liar.

Yeah, Little Red was definitely entering the wolf's den.

Dylan stood behind her, his breath hot on her earlobe. She closed her eyes, feeling his body heat. "If you're looking for drugs, you'll be disappointed. I don't have any."

Dani's eyes flew open, the flame inside her extin-guished. She turned around and took a step back. "I'm not looking for drugs. I thought you may need a friend. I was wrong."

She headed toward the door, but Dylan held onto her arm, tugging her back. "I'm sorry. Don't go."

The solemn tone in his voice pulled at Dani's heart-strings. She wasn't going anywhere. There was something about his blue-gray eyes that held her captive, freezing them in time. She swallowed hard to overcome her emotions and find her words. "How are you?"

"Dani." Frustrated, Dylan shoved his hand through his hair as he turned away. "I don't want any of your psychoana-lyzing bullshit."

"Good, because I'm not going to give you any psychoanalyzing bullshit. I'm genuinely concerned. Jake hit you pretty good."

"It's not broken; I'll live." Dylan sat on the bed, resting his back against the headboard. His long legs were crossed at the ankles. He patted the spot next to him and nodded toward the bed, inviting her to sit. "Come on, Dani, I promise to keep my hands to myself."

Dani knew better than to trust him, but her feet moved on their own accord. She climbed into his bed with her heartbeat racing and sat down next to him. As she leaned back, Dani took in a deep breath. She could do this.

"I'm not going to lie, Dani. After the fight with Jake, I wanted a drink, a smoke, anything to numb my mind. The craving was so strong I forced myself to stay in my bedroom. I said the sobriety prayer, praying that God would grant me the serenity to accept the things I can't change, the courage to change the things I can, and the wisdom to know the difference. I'm not sure I know the difference."

Dylan's raw honesty made her heart ache. She couldn't imagine what he was going through, yet she was proud of him for not taking a drink.

"What if there's something you think you can change, but you're wrong?" Dani felt his hand wrap around hers. "What if you're not in control?"

Dani gripped his hand, comforting him. "I think you do know the difference. Sometimes it's hard to take a step back and realize that you are in control. Dylan, you need to decide if this thing is worth changing. Will this change bring you peace and happiness? If so, you're not wrong for wanting a change."

Dylan exhaled and gazed up at the ceiling. "You make it sound so easy."

"Well, if you drink, the problem will still be there, and

you'd wake up hungover and dehydrated the next morning, hating yourself for wasting ninety days of sobriety."

"Cupcake, you're a fucking genius. How is it that you can put everything into perspective so easily?"

Dani shrugged. "I guess life makes you." She watched their joined hands. Maybe she should take her own advice. She couldn't change her feelings for Dylan. She needed the courage to control them.

Dani turned her head toward Dylan and met his gaze. As he stared into her eyes, she felt as though he was looking at her for the first time. There was a newness that went soul deep. It was an unforgettable moment.

Dylan leaned in. He held her cheek in one hand, caressing it with his thumb. Dani was defenseless and surrendered. She closed her eyes, melting into his touch as his thumb brushed against her bottom lip. *Please, God, don't let him kiss me*, she begged. One kiss would be her undoing.

Dylan's warm breath lingered over her mouth briefly, and her body tensed in anticipation. His lips pressed against hers, and she welcomed the soft and sensual kiss. She felt his hands move to the back of her neck and pull her closer. Goose pimples rose over her skin. God, she didn't want this to end.

Wet and sweet, his tongue slipped past her lips and softly played with hers. Dylan Grace consumed her every thought with what he was doing to her body. She should put an end to this immediately.

He deepened the kiss, feeding a hungering desire they had both been denying. If Dani didn't hold back now, she'd end up sleeping with him. She was that weak.

Dani placed her hand on Dylan's chest, and he stopped, resting his forehead against hers. "We shouldn't do this."

"I know. I'm sorry." Dylan closed his eyes as if it pained him that he'd crossed the line.

"There's nothing to be sorry for. I liked it." Dani cupped his face. "A little too much." She smiled, hoping it would make him feel better.

"You know, Dani, if things were different—" He shook his head. "It doesn't matter."

"What doesn't matter?"

"It's like you said, I'm not wrong for wanting to change the things I have control over." Dylan got out of bed and grabbed a T-shirt lying on a chair. "And I have control over this." He pointed at himself, then to Dani. "We need to stick to the rules."

To say Dani was confused was an understatement. One minute she'd thought he was opening up to her and the next he was cold as ice. She climbed off the bed, feeling cheated of the truth. "Right, let's stick to the rules because it's much easier than talking about our true feelings."

Dylan glared at her. "Dani, you don't want to go there. Trust me."

"See, that's my problem. I do trust you." Before things got out of hand, Dani strode to the door. She turned back to face him. "Since we're sticking to the 'rules.'" Shit, she was using air quotes. "We need to sit down and talk about your goals and how to achieve them." She knew that would strike a nerve.

"Really, cupcake"

"Yeah, it's my job." She whipped out her phone and flipped to her schedule. "Oh, look, I'm free tomorrow. I'll pencil you in." She glared at Dylan as she left the room.

9

*D*ylan crept downstairs. Starving, he headed to the kitchen, praying he wouldn't run into Dani. For the past two days, he had avoided her and her goal-setting session, which was hard to do as they were stuck on the mountain. Since recording had been put on hold because he still wasn't talking to Jake, he'd taken the time to start writing new material, as well as a memoir about life as a rock and roll god. Well, maybe how the god fell. However it turned out, it was a great way to express himself and keep from wanting a fix.

A fix of Dani.

He turned on the kitchen lights. No Dani. Inwardly, he sighed.

Dylan searched the refrigerator and pantry for something to eat, but nothing caught his fancy. He went for an apple as he thought about something to throw together. Maybe he'd bring some food up to Dani.

"Hey."

Dylan turned around, speechless. Dani stood in front of him with her lengthy black hair down and curled, her signature red lipstick on her lips, a white lacy sweater that revealed her white lacy bra, skintight black jeans, and black stiletto ankle boots. What the fuck was going on?

"What?" Dani looked over her outfit. "Do I have something on me?"

"No." Dylan cleared his throat. "No, you just surprised me."

"Good, because it took me all day to pick this outfit out."

"Why?"

"It's a long story."

"I've got time."

"So, you know the Christmas tree I brought home?"

"Yeah."

"Well, it came from a national forest."

"You chopped down a tree inside a national forest?"

"Yeah, I didn't know until I was caught by a park ranger."

Dylan busted out laughing.

"It's funny now, but it was embarrassing. To avoid a fine, I agreed to go out on a date with the park ranger. His name's Ben."

"You're joking, right?" Dylan fought hard to hold back the laughter. "You're being blackmailed by a park ranger?"

"No, you're being an asshole." Dani placed her hands on her hips. "I was flattered that he asked me."

"Wow, Dani, watch the language," he teased.

Dylan sobered under Dani's glare—she obviously didn't like his joke.

Dani was going out on a date. "Do you think that's a good idea? I mean, you don't know the guy."

"We've been texting back and forth."

"Where is he taking you? Do you need a ride? I can go with you and stay in the car in case you need rescuing."

"Dylan, what's with all the questions?"

"I'm concerned." He folded his arms and leaned against the kitchen island.

"I'll be fine. If you must know, I'm meeting Ben at a pub in town for drinks."

Dylan averted his gaze to the floor until she turned around. He peeked up to catch her walking over to the closet to retrieve her jacket. With her ass looking fucking squeezable in those jeans, Ben's hands would be all over her tonight. Lucky bastard.

"Hey." Dani returned, standing right in front of him. "Are you okay?"

Dylan shrugged, passing it off as if he didn't care. "Why wouldn't I be?"

"I don't know. You're acting weird. I can reschedule if you need me to stay."

Thinking about another guy with his hands on Dani was uncharted territory. In the past, whenever he'd wanted Dani, she was there. He'd never worried about another guy. So yeah, the urge to throw her over his shoulder, take her upstairs, and fuck her...claim her...was intense.

"I'm fine. Go have fun."

Dani gave him a smile. "Promise to call me if you need anything?"

"Are you sure that you want me to make that promise because, cupcake, I have a lot of needs."

"Well, rules are rules." She leaned in next to him, grabbing her keys from the island. The sweet scent of roses filled his nose. "No booty calls." She pinned him with a flirtatious grin, then headed toward the door. "Don't wait up."

"Don't do anything I would do," Dylan yelled back as she shut the door.

Christ, don't do anything he would do.

Dani turned back around. "Oh, by the way, I've rescheduled our session for tomorrow. See you then."

"Goodie," Dylan replied dryly.

He watched Dani walk out the door. Maybe this was a good thing. Maybe Ben was what she needed to forget about him.

∼

*T*he scent of evergreen and leather washed over Dani as Ben greeted her with a friendly hug outside the pub. The black leather jacket he wore reminded her of a particular rocker that she wasn't thinking about tonight. Ben was handsome, with his unruly long blond hair freely falling over his broad shoulders. Dani bet he'd worn his best plaid shirt and blue jeans tonight. Who knew lumberjacks were sexy?

The downtown area gave off a quaint mountain town vibe. Storefront log cabins lined the streets. The town's theme was black bears, as Dani had seen driving in. There was at least one bear statue standing outside or inside each store. The shops looked like something she and Melody needed to explore.

Ben opened the door to the pub, and Dani walked in. The warmth from the fireplace in the middle of the room welcomed her. She followed Ben through the dining area, noticing how he knew most of the people in there. Almost every table was occupied, and waitresses were hustling to keep up. The atmosphere was friendly, warm, and welcoming. She liked it.

Ben stopped at a table next to the fireplace and pulled a chair out. Dani smiled. "Thank you." She took off her coat and hung it on the back of her chair before sitting down.

Dani examined the pub as she waited for Ben to take off his jacket and sit down. Before they could talk, the waitress was there for their drink order, and Dani asked for a glass of wine to loosen up.

She didn't date a lot, so she felt a bit awkward.

When they both started to say something at the same time, they laughed. It was apparent; Ben was feeling awkward too.

"You first," he said.

"I was going to say that this place is nice. Good choice."

Ben nodded. "I was going to say that you look beautiful."

Dani eluded his gaze, looking at the table as she blushed. "Thank you." Where was that glass of wine?

An uncomfortable silence followed.

Ben reached across the table and held her hand. "Listen, Dani, I don't want us to feel awkward with one another. Let's just be two friends hanging out."

"I'd like that." Dani flashed him a grin.

"So." Ben leaned forward, resting his muscular arms on the table. "How was your day?"

Ben was racking up all the brownie points—opening the door, pulling out her chair, and now asking about her day. She could get used to that.

"Good."

"Just good?"

"It's complicated."

"Try me."

Dani was careful not to reveal too much out of respect for the band. "I'm a live-in life coach for a rock star who's in town recording new material with his band. So, you can kinda guess how my day went."

Ben looked stunned. "Nonstop parties?"

Dani shook her head. "He's in recovery. I really shouldn't say any more. He's going through a tough time right now."

"I can respect that." Ben stared at her a bit longer as the waitress returned with their drinks.

Dani took a long sip of wine, trying to calm her nerves.

"So, what does a life coach do?"

"Lots of things, actually. For the most part, I help people organize life priorities through goal setting. In this case, I'm also keeping my client sober."

"Wow, that must be tough."

"It is, but my client and I go back a long way. I believe in him and know there's something good out there waiting for him. I want to see him succeed, you know?"

"He's lucky to have someone like you who cares."

Dani shrugged. "I like showing people their true potential."

Their gazes met, and she registered the color of Ben's eyes for the first time. The light was shining just right for her to see a tinge of gray in his blue eyes. *Dylan Grace.*

Dani shook free from the spellbinding stare. She wasn't thinking about Dylan, not tonight. "Hey, enough about me. How was your day?"

"Not as exciting as the day I busted a cute city girl for trying to chop down a sapling in a national forest." He smiled and almost made her weak at the knees.

Dani chuckled. "Very. Funny."

"I enjoyed the text you sent me of the tree decorated in red hearts. I hope your friend appreciated it."

"Yes, he did." Dani saw a glimpse of jealousy on Ben's face. God, she hoped that he wouldn't make this an issue.

"Good." Ben nodded, then changed the subject. "So, tonight is trivia night at the bar, and I thought we could give it a go. That is, if you're interested."

"Absolutely," Dani said with excitement. "I love trivia. Historical? Pop culture?"

"Both."

"Sounds like fun, but I should warn you I'm very competitive."

Ben flashed her another smile. "I like that."

During dinner they loosened up, and conversation flowed. Ben talked about his parents, who were retired and living in Florida, growing up with three older sisters, and his German Shepherd, Roxy. He lived alone near Pine Mountain and hated city life. She mentioned her parents and wasn't shocked when Ben said he had seen the soap opera superstars on TV. He even seemed to be a little starstruck.

After dinner, they made their way to the bar, where they ordered some drinks before trivia started. Game on.

Before Dani knew it, the date was ending. After a wonderful dinner and being crowned the champion of trivia night, Ben walked her to her car.

"Do you think I took it too far?" Dani asked as she adjusted the tiara on her head.

"Too far?" Ben chuckled. "I'm not sure that correcting the quizmaster was wise."

"Well, technically Napoleon wasn't short. He was slightly above average height for a Frenchman of his time."

Ben shook his head and laughed.

They reached Dani's car, and before she realized it, they were saying their goodbyes. She'd had a great time and hated that it was ending. Ben was easygoing and friendly, making her feel comfortable. Definitely good boyfriend material.

"I had a great time, Ben. Thank you."

"I'm glad that you enjoyed yourself." They locked eyes, which made Dani feel awkward. "I'd like to see you again."

Dani looked away, not wanting to hurt Ben's feelings. "As friends?"

Disappointment flashed across his face. "If that's what it takes to see you again."

"Ben, I'm not in a place right now to start a relation-ship. I want to be honest with you. My job is demanding, I start my master's in the spring, and eventually I'll be moving back to LA." And not to mention Dylan Grace, who took up her whole world, but Ben didn't need to know about that.

"Okay." Ben scratched his goatee-bearded chin. "Friends who go out and kick ass on trivia night."

Dani laughed. "Friends."

He opened her car door, and she slipped inside. "Drive safely, Dani. Text me when you get home, so I know you made it."

"I will."

"Talk to you soon."

"Bye, Ben." Dani closed the car door and started up the engine. A part of her didn't want to leave, and part of her couldn't wait to leave. She pulled out of the parking lot and headed toward Pine Mountain, wondering what Dylan was up to. It was midnight. Early for a rock star.

~

*T*o keep his mind off Dani and her date, Dylan invited the guys over for dinner. Before he knew it, he'd cooked a three-course meal and had set the table. However, he was in no mood for Wolf Gang Nude Puck. He kept his clothes on and prayed Dani would too.

Fuck! Dylan shoved his hand through his hair—thank God it was growing back—as he walked into the kitchen. No matter what he did, his mind went back to Dani. Was she having a good time? Did she kiss on the first date?

"Hey," Melody said as she walked into the kitchen with Joe. She hugged him.

"Hey, Mellie."

"God, it smells amazing in here." Melody strode to the stove, inspecting the deep dish he'd just removed from the oven. "Lasagna." She sighed.

"Fuck yeah, dude. Seven layers." Dylan greeted Joe with a fist bump.

"Have you talked to Jake?" Joe asked.

Dylan shook his head. "Not sure I can go there."

"Eventually, one of you will have to apologize."

Dylan found that statement ironic since Joe hadn't apologized for treating him like a child by hiring a life coach. But whatever.

"Hey, motherfuckahs!" Tyler strutted in like he was walking to the beat of his own song. His long, curly, dark hair bounced with each stride.

Dylan gave him a chin up.

"What's cooking? I'm starving."

"Seven-layer lasagna," Melody answered as she made her way over to Joe and stood by his side. Joe pulled her into a hug and kissed her forehead.

"You guys make me sick." Dylan flung the dishtowel he was holding over his shoulder. "Let's eat."

"Wait," Melody said. "Where are Jake and Elliot?"

Dylan shrugged as he grabbed two hot pads, picking up the lasagna.

"Oh, come on. You Grace brothers can hold a grudge." Melody followed him into the dining room.

Dylan placed the lasagna on the table then turned to Melody. "Look, he knows where to find me."

At that moment, the front door opened, and Elijah ran in. Elliot and Jake followed behind. Dylan was the last to congregate into the living room, where everyone was hanging out.

"What's up, little dude?" Joe rustled Eli's hair. "Have you been practicing that fill beat I taught you?"

Eli nodded.

"He's been beating the snot out of the couch pillows." Elliot laughed.

The room fell awkwardly silent as Jake looked at Dylan. "Can we talk?" Jake asked.

Dylan shrugged, acting as if he didn't care either way.

The other bandmates took the cue and brought the gathering to the dining room.

"Look, Dylan, I'm sorry for bringing up Moxley like I did. It was a real dick move."

Dylan folded his arms across his chest, swaying back and forth on his heels as he waited for more apologies.

"I didn't mean to step on your toes. I just wanted to help."

Dylan waved his hand, motioning for more.

"Christ, Dylan, what more do you want?" Jake exclaimed.

"I want to hear from your mouth that I'm the best motherfucking singer/songwriter in the world."

"Fine, you're the best."

"The best what? Come on, Jake, make me proud."

"The best motherfucking singer/songwriter in the world."

"Fuck yeah, dude." Dylan put his arm around Jake as they walked toward the dining room. "I'm positive that my lyrical genius is responsible for a whole lot of pregnancies." He planted a big kiss on Jake's cheek. "And it gets me laid."

"Aw, they made up," Tyler said as the guys walked into the dining room. "It's a beautiful thing. Can we eat now?"

Everyone took a seat at the rustic wooden table. Dylan sat at the head and passed the lasagna to Joe, who was to his right.

"Have you heard the news?" Joe asked, then passed the dish to Melody.

"Heard what?" Dylan asked.

"Davidson is joining us. Mr. Rick isn't pleased with the lack of progress on the album," Joe answered.

"Fuck him." Dylan shook his head. "We don't need him."

"He's bringing Ash," Joe replied.

"I don't think that's a good idea," Melody said as she passed the lasagna to Tyler.

"About time." Tyler dug into the dish twice before handing it to Elliot.

"Pig," Elliot teased him.

"Have you had Dylan's cooking?" Tyler shoved a fork full of cheesy pasta into his mouth.

Melody cleared her throat, gaining everyone's attention. "Maybe Ash should stay in LA."

"Mellie, I appreciate your concern, but I'm okay with it, honestly." For once, Dylan's heart wasn't being ripped out of his chest when someone mentioned Ash's name. He was truly over her. "Besides, I have an idea for a song that Ash would sound amazing on. I was going to run this idea by everyone tonight."

"I'm cool," Tyler agreed as he was more interested in the food on his plate than the conversation.

"Cool with me," Jake said, then looked at Elliot.

"I totally support more women making a guest appearance in the band. The testosterone levels around here are way too high," Elliot said as she winked at Jake.

"How about you?" Dylan asked Joe, wondering what he'd say. Big bro knew all about his toxic relationship with Ash.

Jos shrugged. "As long as Dani can keep you out of trouble."

"Won't be a problem," Dylan reassured.

Dinner had been over a few hours ago when Jake and Elliot had to get Eli ready for bed. The rest of the band stayed longer, shooting the shit. It was midnight and Dani wasn't home yet. Dylan wondered if she was having a good time. Hopefully not too good of a time.

"By the way," Tyler interrupted his thoughts. "Where is Dani?"

Melody shook her head at Tyler, pinning him with a don't ask, wide-eyed look.

"What?" Tyler barked back.

"Seriously, Tyler, read the signs," Melody warned.

"Mellie, it's okay," Dylan reassured. "T, she's on a date."

"Dani's on a date," Tyler sang "Dylan's world has come undone" to the tune of Aerosmith's "Janie's Got a Gun."

Dylan grabbed a thick slice of leftover garlic toast and threw it across the table, smacking the joker in the face. "Fuck you, T. The only reason she's here is because you all don't trust me. I don't need a glorified babysitter."

Tyler looked as if he'd seen a ghost.

"I don't want her here," Dylan continued as Tyler viciously shook his head. "I'm tired of her constantly nagging me about these life-goal sessions. If your purpose was to punish me, job well done." Dylan glanced at Tyler. "And why are you acting like you've seen a ghost?"

Joe leaned into Dylan, looking over his shoulder. "Bro, don't look now; you're fucked."

Slowly, Dylan turned around in his chair. His mouth went dry. "Hey, Dani."

Dani stared back at him, and he swore he saw tears in her eyes. Her cheeks were flushed red, and her lips were pressed tightly together. *Fuck!*

"How was your date?" Melody asked, trying to cut the tension in the room.

Dylan began to sweat as Dani's glare shot straight through him.

"I'll talk to you tomorrow, Mel. Suddenly, I feel ill."

Dylan sat frozen as he watched Dani head toward the stairs. He felt a sharp pain when Joe's elbow connected with his ribs. Dylan was taken aback as his brother gave him a warning glare. "Fix it."

He shot out of the chair and ran after her. "Dani, wait!"

10

"*D*ani, open up!" Dylan pounded on her bedroom door.

"Go away!" Dani yelled.

"Is that the best you can do? Tell me to fuck off. I deserve that much."

She didn't answer, and Dylan couldn't blame her because right now, he couldn't stand himself either. He hadn't meant for Dani to hear him. He'd been trying to get Tyler to shut up. The whole Dani on a date thing had been fucking with his head all damn night. Living in close quarters with a beautiful woman and not touching her was driving him insane. Just thinking of another guy getting to kiss her, fuck her, had sent him off the deep end.

Shit!

Dylan rested his back against the door and slid to the ground. How was he going to fix this? Why couldn't he tell her what he was feeling?

He lazily knocked his knuckles on the door. "Dani, I'm not leaving until we talk. I'll stay out here all night if that's what it takes." Again, silence. "Oh, what was that? You want to hear about my day?" Dylan stretched his long legs, crossing them at the ankles. "Cupcake, that's incredibly nice of you to ask. Let's see. Jake and I kissed and made up. He finally came to his senses and apologized for being a dick. He's like my number one fan now. Really." Dylan kept on, hoping he'd annoy her to the point she'd open the door. "Oh, and I made a chocolate cake with chocolate frosting while you were out on your date. I also made lasagna, but you're shit out of luck on that one. I'm sure it's gone by now. By the way, how did your date go? You're home early. I thought I wouldn't see you until the morning, doing the walk of shame. Inquiring minds want to know, is your Park Ranger more like Grizzly Adams or Gentle Ben? No, I got it, Paul *Bum*-yon."

At that moment, the door flew open, and he crashed backward, smacking his head on the floor.

"Fuck!" Dylan held his head.

"Oh my God, Dylan!" Dani bent down, examining him for an injury. "I'm sorry."

"Me too." He flashed her a devilish smile as he grabbed Dani by the waist, pulling her on top of him.

"Let me go!" She squirmed. "I thought you were hurt." She smacked his chest. "I'm still mad at you."

He let up, but she didn't move. Instead, she held herself up by her arms and glared down at him. He couldn't tell if anger or sadness filled her electric blue eyes. "If you want me gone, just say it."

The weight of her body on top of him made his dick rock hard. Her warmth was like a salve to his soul. His eyes focused on her full lips, and before he knew it, the truth came out. "I don't want you to leave." He brushed back her long black hair from her face.

"Tell me why you want me to stay."

Dylan swallowed. There were a million reason why, but he couldn't tell her one.

"That's what I thought." Dani got up and stood over him, angry and hurt. "How could you embarrass me like in front of everyone?"

Dylan exhaled heavily as he stood up, holding his head. "Dani, I'm sorry. Tyler was busting my balls about you being on a date and I lost my shit…a little. I didn't mean it."

"I've dropped everything to help you." Dani paused as his words finally reached her brain. "Wait." She cocked her head to the side. "You lost your shit because I went on a date?"

"A little," Dylan confessed as he sat on the edge of her bed. There was a war inside his head—confess his feelings or ignore them. "Listen, Dani, I'm not going there with you." He exhaled and flopped back on the bed. "I can't. I shouldn't. "

Dylan felt the mattress give as Dani sat down. "Do you know the first thing I thought about on the drive home from my date?" Her tone had softened.

Dylan shook his head.

"You."

"Dani—"

"No. Dylan, I really care about you. There's something here I can't fight no matter how hard I try. It's always been like this."

"What do you mean?"

"You wreck me, Dylan, every time we are together. I want more."

"Dani—"

"No, you should know. Why do you think I was there all those times you called to hook up? Why I stayed up with you all night talking? It wasn't because of the sex."

"Really? Ouch, that hurts."

"Seriously, Dylan, sometimes you are so clueless."

He wasn't as oblivious as she made him out to be. He just wasn't going there with Dani. Besides, he'd been too fucked up in the past to really notice Dani. Not like he did now.

Yeah, she was his go-to girl. He could zone out and tell her anything...well almost. She knew of his fucked-up upbringing, but not all of it. No one could ever know all of it. That would extinguish his soul.

Dylan shook his head. "You knew the deal, cupcake."

"I know, but it doesn't change the way my heart feels about you. I knew coming here was a mistake. I thought I could handle it."

Dylan slowly rose onto his elbows and gazed at Dani. Her head was down as she fidgeted with the seam on her jeans. A sadness showed on her face that hit him straight in the chest, as if a bullet had impaled his heart. He didn't mean to hurt her, but that's what he did; he hurt the ones he loved. He always did. "What can I do?"

Dani looked up. "You can be honest with me. I deserve at least that much."

She did deserve honesty, but how much was he willing to give? Dylan took in a deep breath and exhaled. "Dani, there are things in my past that have fucked me up forever. My mom is addicted to drugs." He pulled up his shirt, showing off a cigarette burn scar he remembered all too well. "This is what happens, just because."

Dani reached over and touched his scar. "I'm so sorry, Dylan. I've seen those wounds before and I wanted to know how it happened, but you were too high to talk about it."

He looked at her, his eyes vacant. "That happened when I was eight." He took her hand and placed it under his right pec, where his black raven tattoo covered the scar. "Feel that?"

Dani nodded. "The neighborhood bully cut me because he thought I was hiding my lunch money from him. If it wasn't for Joe, I would have had way more ass beatings."

Dylan pulled his shirt down. "Did you know I lived in Melody's dad's maintenance shed until Gracefall went out on our first tour?"

Dani shook her head.

"After Joe put my mom's boyfriend in the hospital for beating the shit out of me, Leo secretly took me and Joe in so we wouldn't end up in child protective services. Fucked up, right?"

The broken smile on his face killed her. "Yes, but your past isn't your fault. You still deserve happiness."

Dylan sat up and scooted to the edge of the bed next to Dani. It was just like her to be so goddamn optimistic. She saw life through innocent eyes, and he'd protect that. He wouldn't drag her through his dirty world of drugs and childhood physical abuse. She was better off booking the next flight out and never seeing him again. "The world isn't full of unicorns and rainbows, you know. Everyone has a demon to slay. I happen to have a few more than most. Maybe it's best that you do leave."

Silence filled the room and sorrow filled his heart. Deep down he didn't want Dani to go, but he had to do what was right.

"This is bullshit," Dani finally broke the silence, her tone catching Dylan off guard. She stood glaring down at him with her hands on her hips. "If you think for one minute that I believe you don't want me here, you are dead wrong. This is you pushing everyone away who cares about you."

Dylan stood and met her gaze straight on.

"Tell me to leave," Dani's voice cracked. Had he defeated her? Did he truly want her gone? He held her cheek in one hand, stroking it gently with his thumb. "I can't."

"Tell me, and I'll go." Tears formed in her eyes.

"Fuck," he sighed and looked away. "Don't leave."

Dani grabbed his chin, forcing him to look at her. "No more pushing me away. Agreed?"

Dylan nodded. Now who was the one defeated?

"And we're doing a session tomorrow morning. Agreed?"

Dylan hesitated.

"Agreed?" Dani pushed.

"Yes, I'll do a session. Just don't cry."

"If crying gets the job done, then I'll do it." She grinned, and that was all Dylan needed to see. Her smile brightened his soul.

Their eyes met, and there it was, that sexual intensity pulling him toward her. His gaze roamed over her full, soft lips. Fuck, he wanted to kiss her. Dani licked her lips, and that was his undoing.

He bent down, and right before their lips touched, Dani took a step back. "I'm not doing this with you."

Dylan's mouth curved up into a smile. "Touché."

"I think we should go to bed. You have an early session in the morning." Dani walked over to the dresser and pulled out a tank top and shorts.

"I'll tuck you in."

Dani spun around and looked at him strangely. "Tuck me in?"

"Yeah." He shooed her off. "Go get dressed and do whatever girls do before bed."

"Okay." Dani reluctantly made her way into the bathroom.

He was out of control. Dylan took a step back and

shoved his hand through his hair. What was he thinking trying to kiss her? If this life coach thing was going to work, he needed to resist.

"I can control this." He leaned his head back, not thinking about Dani's soft, kissable lips. He exhaled. This was worth it. This was worth his sobriety.

Dylan heard the bathroom door open and glanced over. Fuck. There was Dani in her white tank top and black boy shorts. He saw her nipples through the ribbed material. Dylan swallowed hard as she bent over the bed to pull the sheets back. He'd never seen a finer ass.

"Is everything okay?" Dani asked. "You're acting weird again."

Dylan removed his rock T-shirt and tossed it to Dani. "You need to put this on."

"Why?" She looked at him oddly.

"Because my mind will be on your tits all night."

Dani shook her head and put the T-shirt on. She lifted her arms, presenting her new pjs. "Better?"

"Much." But not really. Dani's body was his worst addiction. Here, he didn't have the drugs to tempt him, but Dani... he couldn't escape her.

Dylan watched her climb into bed and pull the sheets up. He tucked her in good and tight, soaking in the way her body felt.

"I think I'm good, Dylan."

He gazed down at her. Long dark hair splayed over her pillow; vibrant blue eyes pulled him in. He was fucked. Dylan bent down and kissed her forehead. "You have no idea how bad I want to slip under those covers and fuck you right now."

He watched her blush.

"I think we should add a rule," Dani said. "Rule number

four, no more talking dirty. It helps reinforce rule number three, no sex. Then again," Dani sat up. "We never clarified the no sex rule. Does it mean no oral sex, sex toys—"

"Dani, stop it."

"I need clarification."

"Go to sleep. I'll see you tomorrow."

Dani laid back down. "Sweet dreams, rock god."

The woman pulled on his strings to the point of fraying. Dylan shook his head as he headed for the door. He turned the lights off as he left. Why did this have to be so complicated?

11

*A*fter a restless night with Dylan on the brain, and not in a professional way, Dani was up early to start a meditation secession as she waited for him. She found the perfect spot on the back deck in the sun. Breathing in the cool mountain air, she took in all the inner peace she could get. Today, the hard questions came for Dylan. There was something evil tormenting his soul, preventing him from being the best Dylan Grace. If he didn't face these demons, Dani was afraid he'd relapse.

Dani finished meditating. Feeling rejuvenated, she looked at her watch; an hour had passed. Where was he? Was she being stood up again?

Keeping with her inner peace, Dani decided to check Dylan's socials and schedule. As she scrolled through his social media pages, she found pictures of Dylan and Ashely Monroe together after shows and at the beach. They painted a picture of a time he had been happy. And why wouldn't he be? Ashely was gorgeous, with her long, red hair, killer body, and a smile that would make a grown man weep. Yeah, Dani was way out of her league.

After one post of them kissing in Paris with the caption "#livingthedream," Dani shut the laptop down. The professional side of her knew Ashely was a trigger and Dylan needed closure. The jealous part of her wanted to delete every post and erase Ashely from his life. She wanted to be living the dream.

Needing a distraction, Dani picked up her phone and quickly checked the time again...two hours late. She inhaled, deeply channeling her fading inner peace. Maybe something had come up. Dani flipped open the scheduler on her phone. Davidson had booked the band tonight at a local club, but that wasn't until later. Where was Dylan?

She had run out of patience. With her yoga pants, gray hoodie, and hair up in a messy bun, she headed inside to find him.

Freshly brewed coffee hung in the air as Dani made her way to the kitchen. After a cup or two, she'd be in a better mood. Then again, she doubted it. No one liked to be stood up.

As she approached the kitchen, she saw Dylan sitting at the island, writing in a leather-bound journal. Dani walked past him to the coffee machine, not saying a word. She was pissed and in no mood for his excuse as to why he'd ditched her this morning.

"Morning, cupcake," Dylan replied without looking up from his notebook.

Seriously? She rolled her eyes as she fixed her coffee with several splashes of vanilla creamer, sipping it until it was perfect. God, she loved a good cup of coffee.

Cradling her mug in both hands, she walked over to the island and stood in front of Dylan, ready to give him a piece of her mind. But she paused as he drew her in. Only wearing jeans, he sat on the barstool in deep thought; his strong jawline twitched a few times as he wrote. There was something to be said about observing Dylan in a different light. Yes, she'd seen his rocker side, but she hadn't seen the creative side of him. It was sexy.

Her eyes roamed over his tattooed chest and the scars he'd showed her last night. It had been a step in the right direction. Perhaps she was getting closer to decoding Dylan Grace. He had suffered as a child, which explained the drug and alcohol abuse. How much he had suffered, she didn't know, but she expected the worst.

"Dani, you're doing it again."

"Doing what?"

Dylan looked up from his notebook. "Looking at me like...you know."

"I'd think that, being a rock star, you'd be used to girls looking at you with crazy eyes."

"Those girls I can fuck. You're off limits."

"Right." She sipped her coffee, enjoying the rich vanilla flavor. "Actually, I was wondering why you stood me up this morning. You were supposed to meet me for a session."

"Fuck, cupcake, I forgot."

"You forgot?" Dylan hit her last nerve.

"Yeah, I forgot." His voice sounded defensive. "Christ, I don't see why this is a big deal. I've fucking told you all I'm going to say."

"Are you serious?" Dani placed her coffee cup on the island a little bit harder than she'd meant to. The blonde brew splashed from the cup and onto his journal.

Dylan frantically flung the notebook, shaking the coffee from it. "What the fuck, Dani?"

"Good. I've got your attention." Dani felt bad, but she pushed forward, squaring her shoulders as she went toe to toe with Dylan Grace. "My time is valuable, and I don't appreciate people wasting it. I'm here to help you, but I won't be disrespected."

Dani turned on her heels and walked away. She didn't make it far before Dylan grabbed her arm. Her body crashed against his. She looked up into smoldering gray-blue eyes that rendered her speechless.

"I'm sorry." His harsh gaze pierced straight through her. Before she could resist, Dylan claimed her mouth. His tongue slipped past her lips and danced with hers like they hadn't skipped a beat. Her hands flew to his chest, but instead of stopping him, she ran them down his muscular stomach, remembering how good he felt.

This wasn't professional—Dylan was her client. But this was very much personal.

He pulled back and cupped her face as she caught her breath. "Honestly, I forgot. After our talk last night, I couldn't sleep, so I stared writing and I haven't stopped. I lost track of time."

Dylan was talking, but Dani couldn't hear a thing over her rapidly beating heart.

"Forgive me?"

Shocked speechless, Dani nodded.

Dylan released her, yet she was still spellbound. She touched her lips where the familiar taste of him still lingered.

He walked over to the island and picked up his journal. "Oh." He whipped around. "Davidson and Ash are here."

"Wait, what?" Dani came back to life. The one woman she'd never met yet hated was here?

"Davidson's here to kick our asses into gear." Dylan rolled his eyes. "Ash and I are going to record a song."

Before Dani could catch herself, she blurted out what was on her mind. "I don't think that's a good idea."

Dylan's brows pinched together as he glared at her.

"I mean, you two had a toxic past. Is this good for your recovery?" Dani didn't say what she really meant. Yes, she was very concerned about their past relationship, but there was something else. Ash was the woman who held Dylan's heart.

"Ash and I are cool," Dylan reassured.

Dani wasn't buying it. "I don't think it's a good idea."

"Why? Are you afraid she'll bring me drugs?"

"If she cared about you, she wouldn't."

Dylan studied her for a moment, making her feel uncomfortable in a good way. "I think there's something else."

"I don't know what you're talking about."

Dylan shrugged. "Whatever, Dani."

"I'm confused. Just because I think Ash being here is a terrible idea, I'm the bad guy? I've seen you lose it when she's around, and I've seen you knock Davidson out because of her."

A smile spread across his lips. "Yeah, I knocked that motherfucker out."

"Not the point. Are you capable of being in the same room with Davidson and Ash and not lose it?"

"Dani, I told you Ash and I are cool. Trust me." He put his arm around her, moving her toward the basement door leading to the studio. "I'll be on my best behavior."

"That's what I'm worried about."

"Besides, I want you to meet Ash."

No way!

"I don't know. I have a lot of work to do." It was a lie. She took a quick look at her clothing; there was no way she was meeting Ash looking like this.

Dylan stopped at the studio door. "I think you should.

You know, make sure I'm being a good boy." He winked with a crooked smile.

"Dylan, trouble always finds you."

"True. All the more reason why you should come."

Dani rolled her eyes. She couldn't say no. Whatever Dylan wanted, Dylan got. "Fine. I'll go grab my laptop and be down in a second."

"That's my cupcake." He smiled, then opened the door and walked downstairs.

For some reason, being called Dylan's cupcake made her feel giddy inside.

A short time later, Dani found herself descending the stairs to the studio with her laptop. She'd just enough time to brush out her hair, put on some lip gloss, and change into a pair of jeans before Ash arrived. The string to her hoodie bounced against her chest. Shoot, she'd forgotten to change her top. She placed her laptop on the coffee table as she heard beautiful music coming from a piano. She followed the tune into a separate room where Dylan was sitting behind a grand piano, playing a soft, flowing melody. His fingers moved gracefully over the black and white keys, each note playing on her heartstrings. The eerie skull tattoos on his hands were a stark contrast to the beautiful music he was playing. Hard lines creased his face as he focused on the song. Dylan was rocker perfection, from his simple white T-shirt to his ripped Levis to the tattoos covering his arms.

Dani leaned against the doorway leading into the studio, losing herself in the song. In her time here, her favorite thing to do was to watch Dylan work. There was a calmness to him, like his music soothed the inner beast. He'd opened up to her a little bit the night before, and she hoped she could get him to say more, to face his demons. Dani had seen him at his worst, and she believed the best was yet to come.

A female voice started to sing, and it pulled Dani away from her thoughts of Dylan. She hadn't noticed the gorgeous redhead holding sheet music and walking toward the piano where Dylan was sitting. Dani's heart sank. Ashley Monroe. The woman she envied. Ash was gorgeous, with her lengthy, full, red hair and bright blue eyes. Her black leather miniskirt showed off her long legs, which Dani imagined had been wrapped around Dylan's waist many times. She was flawless.

Dylan and Ash gazed at each other as they sang. Her voice was smooth, yet it had a raspy rock and roll tone. Their connection was undeniable.

Dani wasn't the jealous type, but she couldn't erase the thought of Ash under Dylan Grace's bedsheets, loving him, satisfying his every need. Moaning sweetly in his ear. Yeah, by the way Ash moved her toned body, she could bring a man to his knees. Dani wished she had a drop of Ash's magic touch, then maybe she would have a fighting chance with Dylan.

Dani wasn't Ash. Whatever the magic was, she needed to stop comparing herself to Dylan's ex. Ashley was an ex for a reason.

It hurt too much watching them together. She had to leave.

As Dani turned to go, she dropped her phone. The crash echoed through the studio, and Dylan stopped playing. "Oh, hey, cupcake." He got up from the piano bench and started toward her. Ash's eyes were on Dani, surely judging her. God, she wished she would have changed her clothes and put on makeup.

"Cupcake?" Ash smiled as she followed Dylan over.

"That's cute." Her tone was condescending. At least, that's how Dani took it.

"Dani, this is Ash," Dylan introduced.

Dani shrugged further into her hoodie as she stood before her girl crush. Ash took the lead and held out her hand. Dani hesitated. Up close, Ash was even more stunning and intimidating.

Dani had heard a lot about her through Dylan when they hooked up. It had been Dani who was there for him when he'd needed a friend. Listening to him putting Ash on a pedestal had been hard. She'd heard it all—how Ash was the only woman for him, how he'd never love again, how Ash was a ho. Well, maybe the latter made her smile a bit. Still, she had heard all the details, good and bad.

"Dani." Dylan looked worried as he studied her. "Are you okay?"

Dani came to and shook her head.

"You're not okay?" Dylan stepped in front of her and grabbed her shoulders. "What's wrong?"

"What?" Dani looked at Dylan strangely. "Nothing is wrong."

"You shook your head when I asked you if you were okay. What's going on?"

Dani exhaled, embarrassed that she'd spaced out. "I'm sorry. I was blown away by your song," she lied. Yes, she loved the song, but she wasn't about to confess she'd been Ash-struck. "I'm sorry."

"It's a great song." Ash playfully hit Dylan's arm. "You have a hit on your hands." She beamed at him knowingly with a smile only they shared. Dani cringed, feeling the bile rise up in her throat.

"Aren't you Melody's friend?" Ash asked.

"Yes."

"I thought you looked familiar. You're Dylan's life coach as well?"

"Yes." God, was that all she could say?

"I know Dylan. You have your hands full." She flashed Dylan a sultry smile.

"I've heard a lot about you too." Dani reached down into her bitch arsenal and retaliated. "Don't worry. All good." She faked a smile.

Ash's condescending tone was irking Dani. What was Ash trying to prove? That Dani got the job because she's Melody's best friend? That she didn't know Dylan the way Ash did? Or maybe Dani made Ash out to be the bitch so she could hate her. No one was that perfect.

"All good? I doubt it," Ash added. "It's a good thing Dylan and I have kissed and made up." Ash gazed playfully at Dylan.

"So, where's Davidson?" Dani asked.

"He's at the cabin working."

"Ah, when the cat's away, the mouse will play."

"Dani," Dylan scolded.

"I should get back to work." Ash left, walking back to the piano.

Dylan glared at her. "Bitchy much?"

"Me?" Dani placed her hand on her chest like she was offended.

"What's going on? You're acting weird."

"No, I'm not. I'm fine." Dani folded her arms.

"Whatever. I don't want to fight."

Dani shrugged. "Who's fighting?"

"Are you staying? I'd like it if you did."

She asked herself why. Why did Dylan want her to stay and watch him with his ex? Was this some kind of kink he got off on? Her job was to make sure Dylan didn't do something stupid, and hooking up with Ash was the definition of stupidity. With her here, Dylan had to be on his best behavior.

"Yeah, I brought my laptop, so I can get some work done."

Dylan flashed her a sly smile. "I promise I'll behave."

"Right, I'll be watching you."

"Good."

Dani inspected him as he walked away. Dear God, the man knew how to wear a pair of Levis.

12

"*A*gain, can someone tell me why we're here?" Dylan asked as he lazily reclined in a chair backstage in his dressing room. He leaned his head back and stared at the cream-colored ceiling with yellow stains that looked like remains of a roof leak, which explained the musky smell. Irritated, Dylan rocked the chair from side to side. How in the hell had Gracefall ended up playing clubs again when they had toured the world's biggest arenas?

"Davidson thought it would be good for band moral." Joe drummed on a makeshift drum pad, a pillow. "You know, playing clubs. Going back to our roots."

What the fuck did Davidson know? Dylan closed his eyes and inhaled. In with the good air, out with the bad. He was irritable and ready to go off. Where was Dani? He needed her. Tonight was the first time he'd perform sober. Yeah, he was on edge.

Dylan was proud of himself, this staying sober thing. Once he'd made his mind up, it wasn't too bad. He sometimes craved a drink or toke, but he realized that it wasn't because he enjoyed any of it. Quite the opposite. He hated the taste of liquor, and the smell of drugs never appealed to him either. Most of all he hated what it represented—a way to escape and numb the pain.

None of this would be possible if it wasn't for Dani. Who'd have known? Lately, he and Dani had been having deep discussions, as friends, and he'd been revealing some shit to himself that actually made him feel better, more confident.

"All I know is if I see another black bear statue, I'm blowing that shit up," Tyler complained as he downed a preshow beer.

Dylan slowly turned his head toward Tyler. "Do you really need an excuse to blow shit up?" He rolled his eyes.

Tyler tipped his beer bottle, agreeing.

The door opened and Dylan turned his attention to Elliot as she walked into the room smiling, wiping the sides of her mouth. Jake strolled in behind her, grinning like a fool and adjusting his fly. Yeah, Dylan knew exactly what had gone down, or better yet, who went down.

"Fuck!" Dylan sat up and scrubbed his face. "I can't do it!"

Joe stopped drumming mid-beat. "What?"

"I NEED to get laid."

Joe laughed. "Now you know how it feels to be cock-blocked."

"Real funny, asshole." Dylan couldn't help but smile a little as he recalled the many times he'd interrupted Joe and Mel's sexy time. Karma was a bitch.

"Maybe it's time we loosen the reins." Tyler stretched out on the couch along the back wall of the dressing room. Given the multiple stains and holes, who knew what was living between the cushions?

"See." Dylan pointed to Tyler. "A man who knows mercy."

"Nope." Tyler shook his head. "I'm tired of your bitchin'."

"Just keep focused on your sobriety." Joe continued the beat. "Everything else can wait."

"Tell that to my dick," Dylan huffed.

"Is this because Ash is in town?" Elliot asked as she sat in front of a mirror, brushing her long blonde hair out.

"No," Dylan snapped. "We're cool."

"It's Dani," Tyler added. "I'd fuck her."

"T, shut the fuck up." Dylan grabbed the pillow Joe had been beating on and threw it at his bass player. "And don't talk like that about Dani."

"Listen, no sex," Joe said. "The band is counting on your sobriety. You fail, we all fail. Dani's doing a good job keeping your ass in line. Don't fuck it up."

Joe stood and clasped his brother on the shoulder. He didn't need to say a word. Dylan knew what he was thinking by the glare in his eyes. However, there was still mistrust hovering between them. Dylan needed to fix that.

A light knock tapped on the dressing room door. "Hey, it's me."

Dylan's heart skipped a beat as he recognized the voice. *Dani!* And since when did he have a heart malfunction? He opened the door. Instead of inviting her in, because he'd had enough of the guys busting his balls, he stepped outside in the hallway.

"Hey." He shoved his hand through his hair. "What's up?" He kept it casual. No, she didn't look sexy at all in her little black sleeveless dress, black leather jacket, and black...*fuck me*...stilettos.

She gazed up at him; her smokey eyeshadow and red

lips accentuated her beauty. He resisted the urge to run his hands through her long, neatly curled hair and pull her into a kiss. Dani looked like she belonged at the side of a rock star. Just not this rock star.

"I wanted to check on you." Dani paused, allowing Dylan to adore the way she was biting her bottom lip. "We didn't get a chance to talk before we left. This is your first show playing sober. How are you feeling?"

Dylan wouldn't lie to himself. He was terrified. He couldn't remember a time when he hadn't been hyped up on something on stage. Would he still perform the same? Would he still have his rocker edge? In the past, he'd drunk to calm the nerves, shot up to play the rock star, and had sex to loosen up. It was bullshit. The drugs, the high, were all a cover. He knew it, Dani was catching on, and he was going to start manning up to it. But fuck! How was he going to handle this newfound clarity?

"I'm good." He lied for Dani's sake. It gutted him knowing she worried about him. He hated that he'd caused everyone around him to worry.

She smiled, buying the lie. "You look good."

He popped the collar on his leather jacket, then ran his hands down his bare chest. "I am a rock god, aren't I?"

"And just when I thought your ego couldn't get any bigger," she teased.

"That's what you get for jumping in bed with fame."

She shifted her weight and folded her arms over her chest. "We agreed to be friends, yes? Let me be your friend."

"Right." He flashed her a wicked smile as he thought about her naked. Dani was exactly the distraction he needed. He caressed her chin. "Cupcake, thank you."

Dani's brows pinched together. "For what?"

"For being here. For giving a shit."

"Of course."

They gazed at each other. Dylan lost himself in a fantasy of happy ever after. Being in this moment when nothing mattered but Dani was priceless. A man would give up his soul to have a woman look at him like Dani was looking at him right now. He should look away, but he couldn't.

She made him feel like he could achieve it all...with her.

Dude, philosophical shit!

Dani averted her gaze. "Are you sure you're okay?"

Dylan nodded, shaking his head and getting back in the moment. "Yeah, more than. I'll catch up with you after the show."

"Yep, I have a front-row seat." She smiled.

"Good, I'll be looking for you." He caressed her chin and winked.

∼

*D*ani made her way back to the main floor of the club. Melody and Ash were sitting at a table next to the stage, drinking champagne. Dani's smile faded into a frown when she saw Ash in her red mini dress, flawless as usual. Why was she here?

Dani faked a smile as she met up with her best friend.

"How's Dylan?" Melody asked. She, too, was looking like rocker arm candy in her black silk, plunging V-neck jump-suit. Dani was definitely borrowing that ensemble.

"He's good." Dani couldn't stop the smirk from forming when she saw Ash's sour expression. "So, Ashley, where's Davidson?"

"Oh, he's over there." Ash pointed at a table in the back where Davidson was sitting with another man deep in conversation. "He's doing business."

Dani could only imagine what kind of deals were going down. According to Dylan, Davidson had high ambitions and didn't care who he screwed over. What did Ash see in him? Yeah, he was handsome, but there had to be more than just looks.

"I hope after tonight the guys can get their shit together and start recording again," Ash said as she sipped her champagne. "The world needs a new Gracefall record."

Dani faked a smile as she grabbed a full champagne flute. "Is this yours?" she asked Mel.

"No." They shared a knowing look between besties. Melody clicked her glass against hers. "Drink up."

"Fuck yeah." Dani took a sip then realized what she had just done.

Melody looked at her wide-eyed. "You are spending way too much time with Dylan."

Ash's giggle didn't go unnoticed.

"I can't believe I said that." Dani laughed.

"So, how is that working out, Dani?" Ash asked as she flipped her long, neatly curled, red hair over her shoulder. It was a nonchalant move, yet it still irritated Dani. She really wanted to ask Ash was why she was here.

Dani played it cool. "It's going well." She sipped her champagne, knowing she was just having this one. She didn't want to be tipsy or under the influence if Dylan needed her later. Technically, she was still on the job.

"I can't see Dylan being okay with a life coach following him around all day. It's like having a glorified babysitter." Ash looked at Dani. "No offense."

"None taken," Dani lied. It killed her that Ash knew Dylan on a personal level that she hadn't experienced yet. Yes, Dani was his go-to girl in LA, but she'd never dated him; she'd never had that connection and probably never would. But Christ, she wanted to reach across the table and slap that smirk off Ash's face. "Dylan wants my help, and as long as he does, I'll be there for him."

"Good luck with that. Dani, don't be naive. Don't mistake him for a dream. He's a one-way ticket to the dark side." Ash pursed her lips together as if she had more to say but wouldn't. Good thing. Dani didn't want to hear another word from her mouth.

Ashley didn't know what she was talking about because she knew the old Dylan. Another reason why he didn't need to be around her. Note to self: that's why you don't like Ashley—aside from the fact that she was lovers with your client...something Dani wanted to be.

"I can take care of myself. Besides, it's not like that. Purely business."

"It's always like that with Dylan." Ash took a sip of champagne as she glared at Dani from over the brim of her glass.

"Oh, look." Melody glanced toward the door. "Cherry and Tomi are here."

Dani was thankful for the distraction. She needed to evaluate this conversation later because there was something deep there, and she was sure it had more to do with Ashley than Dylan.

"So," Melody said as they waited for their friends to make their way through the crowd. "I found a wedding photographer."

"Who?" Dani asked as she ordered a Diet Coke from the waitress.

"Cherry's sister, Tomi."

Melody flipped through her phone and showed her Tomi's social media page. "She posted some sneak peek photos of the guys. Isn't she amazing?"

Dani scrolled through the images and stopped on one of Dylan sitting behind the piano, singing. It was black and gray, which matched his mood. Tomi had captured his gracefulness and rocker edge perfectly. He was perfection. "She's amazing."

"I know, right?" Melody slipped her phone back into her pocket. "Tomi's photographing the show tonight."

"Have you noticed the way Tyler looks at Tomi?" Dani asked. "I think he likes her."

Melody shook her head. "For Tyler's sake, he'd better stay far away from Tomi. Cherry will castrate him if he even thinks about touching her younger sister."

"Hey, ladies," Cherry greeted as she and her sister sat down at the table. "Oh, Dani, I'm so glad that you are here. I've been meaning to give these to you." Cherry reached into her purse and pulled out a pair of pink, fuzzy handcuffs. "Here." Cherry handed the cuffs to Dani. "You may need these."

Melody busted out laughing, which confused Dani. "You will definitely need them."

Ash smirked as she stood. "Seriously, Dani, good luck with Dylan." She sauntered off toward Davidson.

Dani didn't like being the butt of the joke. She held up the cuffs like they were contaminated. "I don't understand."

"They're for Dylan," Melody said, causing Dani to blush. "Oh."

"Not like that," Cherry laughed. "Use them when Dylan gets out of control. Handcuff him to keep him out of trouble."

Dani looked at Melody. "Did you use these on Dylan when you managed their tour last summer?"

Melody nodded. "Trust me, keep them close by."

Dani studied the handcuffs then put them in her purse. What had she gotten herself into?

"It's time." Melody beamed.

Excitement raced through Dani's body as they made their way to the front row. The band wasn't even on stage, yet the electricity of anticipation was in the air. Dani couldn't wait to see Dylan onstage rocking his leather pants.

"Dani?" a man with a deep voice called behind her.

She turned around. "Ben!"

"Hey." He pulled her into a friendly hug. "I had no idea you'd be here."

Ben let her go, and she took a step back, adjusting her dress. "Yeah, I'm kinda working."

"Hi. I'm Melody." She held out her hand, and Ben shook it.

"Ben."

Melody looked at Dani with a knowing grin. Dani shot her a *don't you dare embarrass me* glare.

"So, you're working here?" He looked her up and down, questioning her outfit like she should be wearing a waitress uniform.

"I'm with Gracefall. This is the job I was telling you about. I'm the lead singer's life coach. I'm here for support."

"Really? I'd heard that the lead singer had been in rehab."

"Yeah, but he's doing really well now."

"That's awesome. Gracefall wouldn't be the same without Dylan Grace."

Dani nodded. "The show is about to start. I should get back to my friends."

"Yeah, I should get back too. How about we get a drink after the show?"

"I'm not sure how things will go but I'll text you if I'm free."

"*F*air enough." Ben smiled. He had a great smile —broad, friendly. "Hope to see you soon."

Dani smiled back and watched him walk away. Ben was kind, handsome, and boyfriend material. Why couldn't she have fallen for someone ready, willing, and able to have a relationship? Ben was a great guy, just not the guy for her.

"He's cute." Melody stood next to her.

"Yeah, look at all that long untamed blonde hair," Cherry added.

Dani rolled her eyes. "It's not like that. We're friends."

"Um, no way. Not the way he looks at you." Melody turned back toward the stage.

"Mel, I'm not interested. Besides, I'm too busy. Tonight I'm focused on Dylan. You know, this is first time he's performed sober."

"And I'm glad that he has you...as a life coach. But you need to live your life."

"I know." And Dani did. She wasn't about to inform her best friend that she'd gotten behind on her online classes.

The lights dimmed, and Dani's heart raced with excitement like it always did when Dylan was on stage. The crowd cheered and chanted, "Gracefall! Gracefall!"

Dylan walked toward the mic stand through the smoke billowing over the stage. "We're fucking Gracefall," he growled into the mic; his voice vibrated through her body, turning her on.

The fans screamed. For a small venue, it felt like a packed arena.

Dylan looked behind him at Joe, and they shared a nod

before Jake's riff screamed out. The spotlight fixed on Dylan standing behind the mic, looking like a rock god in his leather jacket, tattooed and pierced body, and black leather pants. He closed his eyes, taking in the music as he wrapped his hand around the mic and began to sing. His rough, raspy voice was rocker perfection.

"I fell from grace when you left
A void in my heart I can't erase
Let's be honest, you never cared in the first place
Now I know I'm visiting darkness."

The tempo gradually escalated to full, raw, in-your-face heavy rock. Dani closed her eyes and swayed to the music, feeling the tone of Dylan's emotional lyrics. She'd seen the guys play "Visiting Darkness" a few times, but now knowing about Dylan's past, she understood the song better.

Dani opened her eyes to find Dylan looking at her as he sang.

"Visiting darkness, come inside
Visiting darkness, my peace of mind
Visiting darkness, my time is up."

Her throat went dry under the intensity of his stare. The music held her body captive, moving to the beat. Now she understood why Dylan had a huge fanbase. He connected with people.

The set continued. The crowd went crazy over Gracefall's remake of Duran Duran's "Hungry Like the Wolf." She even danced with Melody like crazed fans. When the hour set came to an end, the guys took a bow and left the stage.

She followed Melody to the VIP room in the back of the club, where they would meet up with the band and a few close friends. Cherry and Tomi were already waiting for them at the table. Dani took off her jacket and hung it on the back of her chair as Melody sat down.

"Here's a sneak peek." Tomi handed her camera to Dani. "I've never met someone as photogenic as Dylan."

Dani scrolled through the photos, reliving the show. Butterflies fluttered in her stomach as she took in one image of Dylan giving her a wink. With that sultry grin and wink combo, no feeling came close to how Dylan made her feel. "The guys are going to love these." Dani returned the camera.

"I hope so," Tomi said as she looked through the pictures. "I can't wait to get these uploaded."

The fans in the VIP room came alive, gathering at the entrance. Dani looked toward the door, and Joe led the rest of Gracefall into the room. Dylan was last and looked as if he'd just showered.

Excitement coursed through Dani's body as she waited for Dylan. Still pumped from the show, she couldn't wait to wrap her arms around him, take in his clean male scent, and hang out with rock stars for the rest of the night. Tonight, she loved her job.

Joe made a beeline straight to Melody, picking her up and twirling her around in a hug. They kissed each other like they were the only two in the room.

Jealous much?

Jake and Elliot joined them. They, too, still had adrenaline coursing through their veins as they talked about the show with Cherry and Tomi.

Tyler was next. He took a long swig from a bottle with amber liquid, then spit-sprayed it over them. Lucky for Dani, she wasn't in the line of fire.

Everyone had settled into a booth, talking and drinking like old friends. Dani sat alone at the table, fading into the background. She scanned the room for Dylan. Instead of making his way to her, he'd made his way to Ash. Dani's heart plummeted. The bitter reminder that she'd never be significant enough to fit into Dylan's world set cold into her grim reality. Here she was sitting and drinking her Diet Coke alone, waiting for Mr. Rock God to come sweep her off her feet.

Pathetic.

Dani sipped her drink as she tortured herself, watching Ash lean in close to Dylan, teasing smiles and all. God, she felt like an idiot. Why was she even here? Oh yeah, it was her job.

As things looked, Dylan had everything under control. Ash was going home with him tonight, which made Dani uneasy. Dylan had worked too hard for Ash to come along and mess everything up. Dani had to keep her eyes on Dylan, but it didn't mean she had to do it alone.

Dani pulled out her phone and texted Ben.

Dani: Up for that drink?

She waited for what seemed like forever for Ben to respond. The gray text bubble appeared, and she relaxed.

Ben: Yes. Where are you?

Dani: VIP room. I'll meet you outside in five?

Ben: On my way.

As she put on her jacket, Dani shoulder her way through the crowded room to the entrance. She stepped outside into a packed hallway, where Mac was manning the door.

"Ms. Clark," he greeted.

"Hey, Mac." Dani looked down the hallway, searching for her lumberjack. "Dylan's inside."

"I know. I'm looking for a friend."

"I see." Mac was at least six foot six and towered over Dani. "What does he look like? I have a better vantage point up here."

Dani laughed. "Very funny. He's about your height, long wavy blond hair. Kinda looks like a lumberjack."

Mac looked over the crowd. "Is that your guy?" He pointed to Ben.

"Yes. Can you wave him this way?"

Mac nodded and waved to Ben.

In no time Ben had made his way to her. He looked sexy with his hair down, wearing a plaid shirt over a white T-shirt and jeans.

He greeted her with a big hug. "Hey."

"Hey." A flirtatious grin spread across her face as she took his hand and led him inside the VIP room.

"So," Ben yelled over the loud music. "We get to hang out with rock stars tonight."

Dani looked over her shoulder at Ben. "We sure do."

And she wasn't going to feel guilty about it either. It was time her heart moved on from Dylan Grace.

13

*D*ylan watched Dani walk out of the VIP room, wondering where she was headed. He'd been trying to make his way to her all night. He hated seeing her sitting alone, but he couldn't escape. First, before arriving, the paparazzi had cornered him and Ash, firing questions about their relationship status. Thank God Mac had been nearby and had safely ushered them inside. Just when he'd thought he was in the clear, Davidson had trapped him, introducing him to a couple of friends. The arrogant asshole had gushed over Dylan, using his celebrity status to impress the ass clowns.

Dylan had to get the fuck out of there.

"Listen, D," Dylan interrupted. "You're a real buzzkill right now. I'm out of here."

Dylan didn't stick around for a formal goodbye; he needed to find Dani.

As he made his way it to the door, in walked Dani. He picked up the pace but froze in his tracks when he saw her with a giant of a man. *What the fuck?*

Dylan disappeared into the crowd, never taking his eyes

off Dani. He watched them from afar as they found a high-top table and puked a little inside as he watched the giant man pull her chair out, trying to win her over. Dani took off her jacket and fuck...her breasts were spilling out of her black strapless dress. Mr. Plaid's eyes were all over her. *Fuck that!*

Was this Dani's lumberjack? Dylan sized him up. The dude was a beast, at least six foot five, and built like a brick building. Is this what turned Dani on? Dylan did a quick mental check, noting he needed to add more plaid to his wardrobe and hit the gym.

Dylan cracked his neck from side to side before joining Dani and her friend. The lumberjack wasn't getting Dani without a fight. "Hey, Dani." Dylan pulled up a barstool and joined them.

"Holy shit!" Dani's friend exclaimed. "Dylan Grace."

"Fuck yeah, dude." Dylan nodded.

"Dylan, what are you doing here?" Dani didn't look happy to see him. *What the fuck?*

"Oh, shit, this is a date?" Dylan faked being surprised.

"No," Dani answered quickly. "Friends having a drink. Dylan, this is Ben."

"No shit. You're the park ranger that almost arrested Dani for murdering a tree."

Ben snickered. "No, man, I let her go with a warning."

"A warning? I think blackmail is more accurate." Joking aside, Dylan turned on asshole mode. This guy was a douche. "I mean, a woman like Dani should be asked out properly, not forced."

"Dylan, Ben didn't force me to do anything. Stop it." A hint of red blushed her cheeks. Christ, she was gorgeous when mad.

"I'm sorry, Dani, if you took me asking you out as black-mail." Ben looked confused.

"No, I didn't think that at all." Dani glared at Dylan. "I thought it was sweet."

Sweet? Bile rose in his throat. Dani didn't like sweet. And there was no way she was attracted to Grizzly Adams. "My bad."

"Shouldn't you be getting back to Ash? I'm sure you don't want to keep her waiting." Jealousy gleamed in her eyes, and now Dylan knew what this was all about. He'd suspected that Dani was jealous of Ash, and now it was confirmed.

But what *really* made him want to dance was that it meant she cared—like for real!

"Ash is with her boyfriend."

"Never stopped you before."

Yep, his girl cared. "Fuck, Dani, low blow much?"

"Low blow? You're one to talk. Blackmail much?"

"Hey," Ben interrupted. "Looks like you two have some things to iron out. I should go."

"No." Dani grabbed his hand. "Dylan was just leaving."

"No, cupcake, I think Ben is right. He should go. We have business to take care of. I mean, you are on the clock."

"Dani, I'll text you tomorrow." Ben slipped his hand away. "Have a good night." Turning to Dylan, he added, "Great show, man. It was an honor to see you and Gracefall perform."

Dylan was slightly feeling like shit now and redeemed himself by saying, "Thanks, dude. Appreciate it."

Dani nodded goodbye as the big hulk walked away.

"About fucking time," Dylan huffed. The dude was cramping his style.

"You are unbelievable!" Dani glared at him.

"I'm unbelievable? *You* left me."

"No, you left me alone to watch Ash flirt with you. And from where I stood, you looked to be enjoying it."

"Oh, I get it. This is about Ash." He snickered, confirming that it was just as he'd thought.

"Whatever, Dylan. You're free to have sex with whoever you want. Who am I to stop you?" Dani fell quiet. Hurt washed over her face, and Dylan didn't know what to do. He'd taken it too far.

Classic Dylan move.

He studied her for a minute. There was nothing he could say to make her believe Ash was only a friend. But he could sure as fuck show her. Dylan hopped off the barstool and grabbed Dani's jacket and hand, pulling her up to stand.

"What are you doing?"

Dylan didn't answer as he dragged her to the women's bathroom. He walked in, and a group of women gasped.

"Get the fuck out," Dylan said as he checked the stalls.

"I'm sorry," Dani said to the women as they hustled out. Dani went for the door. "I'm out of here."

Dylan stepped in front of her and locked the door. He laid her jacket on the counter as he stalked up to her. Dani took a step back and hit the wall behind her. There was nowhere to run; he had her right where he wanted her. She shook her head. "No, we are not having bathroom sex."

Dylan nodded. "Yes, we are."

"This is against the rules."

"Fuck the rules, Dani." He wrapped his arm around her waist and pulled her against him. "Tell me to leave, and I will." He slid his hand behind her neck, bringing her lips to his. "Tell me."

Her hands were on his chest, not pushing him away but caressing his muscles. "That's the problem. I can't."

Their lips crashed together in a heated hunger he couldn't contain. He needed Dani like the air he breathed. He needed to be inside her, now.

He picked her up and sat her down on the sink counter. She wrapped her beautiful legs around his waist as he hiked up her dress. With his lips never leaving hers, he slid his hands up her thighs and pulled down her panties, working the black lace past her stilettos.

"Dylan, you're my client. This isn't professional," Dani protested, but her body told him a different story. She wanted him as much as he wanted her.

"You're fired." He leaned her head back, trailing kisses down her neck.

"I've never been fired before," she moaned. "I will need compensation."

"Then consider this your severance package." He winked at her wickedly, then kissed her hungrily as he reached between her thighs, parting her sex with his fingers. Fuck, she was hot and wet and ready for him. "Fuck me, cupcake," he hissed against her mouth.

Dani grazed his bottom lip with her teeth, tugging it gently as she reached down and unbuttoned his pants. "I need you."

He gazed down at her and was met with the sexiest grin. Christ, he loved the lust brewing in her eyes. She took his hard cock in her hands and stroked him, driving his primal instinct to claim her, body and soul.

Dani's hand smoothed over the head of his dick as she stroked him faster, just the way he liked it. Overtaken by her touch, Dylan fell forward, slamming his hands against the mirror. Her touch felt fucking amazing, like magic against his skin. He was so close to coming.

Dylan slipped out of her grasp and slid Dani's ass to the edge of the counter as he worked his pants down to his ankles. She locked her legs around his waist, and he entered her hard and fast, sliding all the way in. Dani gasped and held onto him, digging her nails into his back. Fuck, that sweet first gasp as he entered her tight, wet pussy drove him wild.

Cold stiletto heels pierced his ass as she tightened her legs, pulling him deeper. "Dylan," she moaned.

His name coming from her mouth was unlike any song or melody he'd ever written. If he could make it happen, he'd record that sound and play it nonstop. Was this how it felt to fuck Dani sober? He pulled back, leaving the tip of his dick inside her, then slid back in. The air in his lungs hitched as a mind-blowing sensation captured his body.

Pleasing Dani consumed him, and he pumped her harder. Before he knew it, he'd reached his orgasm and come inside her. As he caught his breath, it only took a second to process what he'd done.

"Fuck." Dylan pulled out and hid his head on Dani's shoulder. "I'm sorry," he panted.

He felt her fingers thread through his hair and caress his head. At least she wasn't punching him. "I'm on the pill." Dani kissed his cheek.

"You're not mad?"

"No, but we should be more careful. I mean, I could've said no."

Dylan stood up. "No, you can't resist me." He flashed her a teasing smile.

"Don't push it." Dylan helped Dani off the porcelain countertop. She adjusted her dress as he pulled up his pants. As she tucked her hair behind her ear, she searched the bathroom floor.

"Looking for these?" Dylan swung her black lace panties around his finger. Dani stepped forward and tried to grab them, but he tightened his hand into a fist, trapping them in his hand. Dylan wrapped his arm around her waist, pulling Dani against him. He bent down and kissed her deeply.

A knock on the bathroom door interpreted them. "Hey, you've been in there long enough," a woman's voice complained.

"Fuck off," Dylan called out as he stared into Dani's eyes. For the first time, he really saw Dani. He saw the woman who brought him to his knees, and he saw the woman who was his everything. It scared him shitless.

Dani giggled. "We should go. We've occupied the bathroom for too long."

Dani's vibrant blue eyes looked straight into his soul. God help him; he needed Dani in his life. He caressed her cheek. "Cupcake, you mean the world to me. I want you to know that."

Dani nodded. "I know."

Dylan smiled as he pulled her into a hug. "So, should I get you back to Benny Boy, or are you hanging out with me tonight?"

Dani put on her jacket, flipping her hair out from underneath it. "I mean, I should find Ben and apologize for my obnoxious friend."

Dylan leaned against the counter and folded his arms across his chest, watching Dani fix her makeup. "Grizzly Adams can take care of himself. Besides, I need you tonight. Don't make me go back out there without you. It would ruin my reputation."

"Your reputation?"

"Yeah, I always have a beautiful woman on my arm."

Dani shook her head.

"Seriously, I want to spend time with you tonight."

Dani faced him, studying him for a moment. "Rock stars are more exciting than lumberjacks."

"Fuck yeah, we are."

Her lust-filled blue eyes rendered him speechless as she looked at him. Her lips were slightly swollen from his kisses, and didn't that make him feel like a sex god? "You still have my panties?"

"You mean these?" Dylan twirled the black lace panties around his finger.

Dani rolled her eyes and held out her hand.

"These are mine." Dylan shoved the underwear into the pocket of his leather pants. "Knowing you have nothing on under that dress is going to drive me fucking crazy for the rest of the night. I'm not letting you out of my sight."

Dani blushed. Christ, how he loved making her blush. She headed toward the door, giving him a flirty grin from over her shoulder.

How could he be so lucky? She looked like sin and felt like heaven in his arms. A good and bad girl wrapped up perfectly as if she'd been made for him. He was in way too deep.

∽

*W*hat the hell had she done? Dani held Dylan's hand as he led her through the crowd of people in the VIP room. Her legs barely kept up with his long stride. The deal was no sex, and she'd messed up, royally.

"I see the guys." Still holding her hand, Dylan headed toward a red booth in the back of the room.

Melody and Joe and Jake and Elliot were sitting at the booth with Tyler. Tyler stood and gave Dylan a bro hug. "You made it finally."

"Yeah, had to take care of some business." Dylan winked at Dani, and she felt her cheeks blush.

God, she hoped no one could see through her guilt as she tried to hide that they'd had sex. Dani slid in next to Tyler, and Dylan slid in next to her. Everyone was jam-packed shoulder to shoulder. Alcohol was flowing, which made her worry about Dylan, but she was relieved when the waitress brought a tray of glasses filled with water. Now, if she could only control her anxiety.

Dylan leaned in and whispered in her ear. "You're nervous."

"No, I'm not," Dani denied.

"Then why are you squeezing my leg?"

Mortified, Dani looked down and, yep, there she was, clenching his thigh. "Sorry. I think they know."

"Know what?" Dylan played it off.

"You know." She looked at him with wide eyes.

"Phfft. Don't worry about it."

She was worried. It wasn't like her to sleep with her clients. She was a professional. "Dylan, this my job."

"I fired you, remember?"

She shot him a glare.

"Fine, you can have your job back. However, you've already been compensated." He winked. "We'll have to rene-gotiate the deal."

"Really?" What was he up to?

"Absolutely. I will no longer be referred to as your client."

"Then what are you?"

"We're friends. Close friends, agree?"

"As long as—"

"No debating. Take it or leave it."

These negotiations were not part of the deal. And did Dylan have the authority to fire her, then rehire her? No, this was classic Dylan, trying to get his way. Since Joe was the one who'd hired her, it wasn't like she could report this to him. That wouldn't go over well. In fact, she would surely be fired for breaking the no sex deal. This was her mess to fix.

"Friends," she agreed.

"Friends with benefits. It's a deal." He raised his glass of water and took a sip, sealing the agreement.

Wait...had she been tricked? Was she back in fuck buddy territory?

"Hey, where did you two disappear to?" Elliot asked Dani.

Dani didn't know how to respond. Her head was spinning, which always seemed to happen when Dylan was around. She couldn't keep up with his sly ways of getting everything he wanted. She didn't have an excuse.

"Did you give her the ole razzle dazzle?" Tyler held out his fist for Dylan to bump and was left hanging.

Dani turned to Dylan, meeting his gaze, waiting for him to respond. "No sex, remember?" He winked. "Since when do I need to report back, T? Dani's with me; I'll be a good boy." This time he smirked wickedly, causing her insides to melt.

Thank God, he had her back.

"What's the ole razzle dazzle?" Tomi asked.

Everyone busted out in laughter.

"What?" Tomi shrugged as she downed an acholic drink.

Tyler put his arm around Tomi's shoulder. "Does your sister know you're here?"

"Yes." Tomi giggled, obviously wasted. "She's somewhere around here."

"Well." Tyler cleared his throat and looked her up and down. "I can show you the ole razzle dazzle."

"T, hands off," Joe warned. "Cherry isn't far. Little sis is off limits."

"Don't worry. She's in good hands." Elliot got up from the booth.

"That's right," Melody added. "Us girls have to stick together."

"So," Joe turned to Melody, confused. "Why do you all go to the bathroom together? I never understood that."

"So we can talk shit." Elliot held out her hand to Tomi. "Come on. Let's go find Cherry. You've had enough to drink."

With disapproval on her face, Tomi got up and followed Elliot.

Dani sat back and took in the scene. AC/DC's "You Shook Me All Night Long" blared through the speakers as the guys shouted over the loud music to one another. Dani saw the brotherhood they shared, and it made her happy to see Gracefall getting along. She tried to join in the conversations, but she couldn't keep up. It was as if all the TV channels were on at once. However, she was only interested in one channel, and he was sitting next to her.

Dylan snaked his arm around her waist and pulled her close. The smell of sex and leather washed over her, reawakening her desire. Leaning in, he nuzzled her neck. Warm breath danced over her skin. "You doing okay?"

"Yeah, always a good time with Gracefall. And you?"

"I can't stop thinking about your pretty kitty." His hand traveled up her thigh.

Dani's breath hitched in her lungs, and she wiggled in her seat.

Dylan smirked, obviously pleased with his effect on her. "You always seem to amaze me, cupcake."

She turned her head toward his, their mouths a breath away. "I aim to please."

Her heart raced as he softly ran his finger down her neck, stopping at the top of her dress. She shivered. "You're shaking."

"Yeah, you kinda do that to me."

"Really?"

She nodded. "Every time you touch me."

He kissed her deeply. Her heart fluttered as she realized that Dylan Grace, the rock star god, was kissing her passionately in public. Was he letting everyone know that she was his? No, it couldn't be. This was her lovesick brain giving her hope that Dylan had changed his mind about relationships.

No, she wasn't a fool. There was no separating business from pleasure, and there wasn't another man she wanted. She wanted to be right here in Dylan's world for however long that might be.

Fool, no.

In love, absolutely.

14

*D*ani sat next to Dylan in the limo as the driver took them back to the cabin. Dylan sat with his long legs crossed comfortably, staring out the window. A distant look loomed over his eyes, making them appear dark. His arms were folded, closing the world out.

Dani wrapped her arm around his. "Hey." She kept her voice low so no one would hear her but Dylan. Not like anyone was paying attention. Joe and Melody were lip locked, Elliot and Jake were absorbed in their cellphones, and Tyler was passed out. "Are you okay?"

Dylan didn't answer.

"Dylan," Dani said louder.

His head snapped toward her. "Yeah?"

"I've been trying to get your attention. Are you okay?"

"I'm fine." Dylan shrugged her off and went back looking out the car window.

Brooding Dylan Grace was one of the many moods Dani had grown to recognize. It was a dark place he visited often, and it broke her heart to see him in pain. She wished Dylan would talk to her. But he wouldn't.

When Dylan was in this dark place, he'd shut the world out. He was numb to everything. If Dani pushed too hard, it would get them nowhere. However, she kept a close eye on him because this was a trigger for him to spiral out of control and self-medicate with alcohol and drugs. It was a vicious cycle. And until he released his demons, he may never be free.

Feeling helpless, Dani's chest tightened. She wished she could take his pain away.

Dani laid her head on his shoulder. "You know you can talk to me, Dylan. I'm your friend."

He kissed her forehead. "I don't have many friends." Dylan unfolded his arms and held her hand.

Dani gripped his hand. No other words were needed. He'd come around in his own time, and when he did, she'd be there for him.

The limo came to a stop, and Dani woke. She was surprised that she'd fallen asleep, given her mind was spinning with thoughts. As she sat up, she pulled her cellphone out and checked the time.

Three o'clock in the morning.

Rock and roll.

Dani got out of the limo and shuffled her way into the cabin. Dylan was a few steps behind. In silence, they made it upstairs, and before Dani went inside her bedroom, she turned to Dylan, wishing he'd kiss her goodnight. With his head down, he mumbled goodnight, then walked into his room.

With just enough energy to walk inside her bedroom and close the door behind her, Dani began her nightly routine. It felt like heaven to kick off her shoes and ditch the mini dress. She put on her pjs then went into the bathroom to wash her face and brush her teeth. As she removed her makeup, she took a long look in the mirror. She didn't recognize herself with the dark circles under her eyes. She was tired. Dani shook it off and pulled her hair back into a ponytail. She paused when she saw a red bruise on the side of her neck. A hickey? She touched it. Since when had she become so reckless?

Dani Clark didn't have sex in a bathroom.

Yeah, but she was a rock star's fuck buddy.

There was a difference, right?

Shit, she didn't know.

Through her inner musings, Dani walked away from her reflection and all regrets.

Dani wasn't ashamed. As long as her reckless behavior didn't land her on the front page of a gossip magazine, she'd be fine. She was always careful not to tarnish the squeaky-clean family name. Until Dylan, Dani had walked the straight and narrow, never disappointing them. She was tired of living up to those expectations.

It felt so good being so bad with Dylan Grace.

Dani pulled the covers back and crawled into bed. With dreams of Dylan in her head, she fell asleep.

Dani stirred as the mattress gave way next to her. A lean figure lay behind her, consuming her half-awake senses with the scent of spice and leather. *Dylan.* Her body reacted on its own as she snuggled against him. If this was a dream, she sure as hell didn't want it to end.

"Good afternoon, cupcake." Warm breath wafted past her ear, giving her skin goosebumps.

She lazily stretched. "Afternoon?"

"You were sleeping so peacefully. I didn't want to wake you." His soft hand slipped under her shirt and squeezed her breasts. "I got impatient."

Dylan left a trail of hot kisses across her jawline and down her neck. She moaned.

"I love it when you make that sound," he whispered in her ear as he rubbed her nipples between his fingers.

Dani's body and mind were at war. Her body was in the *fuck me, please* zone, but her mind was on a different level. "I should probably get up and—" Oh, God, his hand had slipped inside her panties and found her clit. He massaged the sensitive flesh, causing her to throw all good sense to the wind.

"Everyone is still sleeping off last night." He ran his finger down the inside of her sex, giving her clit a break. "But I'll stop if that's what you want."

"Don't you fucking dare." Like the greedy woman that she was, Dani pressed her ass against his cock. One touch and Dylan had her wound up tight and ready to go.

"Language, cupcake," Dylan teased, scolding her. "I have never heard you curse before."

"That's what happens when you hang out with rock stars," Dani said breathlessly.

"Mmm, I like it." His lips were wet on her neck. One hand held her breast captive, sweetly torturing her hardened nipple, while the other was between her thighs rubbing her sex, relentlessly building up her orgasm. "I want to hear you say fuck again, cupcake."

"Fuck," she moaned as her body squirmed from the pleasure.

"That's good, but we can do better. Tell me to fuck you."

Dani couldn't find the words to say. Dylan had her on the edge of coming. "Fuck me, Dylan," she panted.

"So fucking hot."

Dani reached behind her and unbuttoned his pants. To her surprise, they were already undone. She slipped her hand down his pants and gripped his cock. It was hard and smooth and so ready for her. Dylan grabbed her hand. "Ladies come first, cupcake."

Still behind her, he yanked her panties down her thighs, and she shimmied and squirmed, finally working them off. He parted her legs and thrust deep inside from behind. Still sensitive from their earlier bathroom sex, Dani hissed from the sting.

"You okay?"

She nodded and shifted, placing her leg behind her, giving Dylan more access.

He rubbed her clit as he pumped her hard and fast, causing Dani to lose all control. As he increased the rhythm, she grabbed ahold of the wrought-iron bars on the headboard. She was in the fast lane holding on for dear life.

"Come for me, baby." He thrust, persistent in making her shatter into a million beautiful pieces.

Heat flushed her skin, her body quivered. Oh, God, she was coming undone. She held on as Dylan drove her over the edge of sweet oblivion. He didn't let up as she rode out her orgasm to its mind-blowing completion. Dylan's body tensed as she felt his release deep inside her.

With Dylan still inside, they lay there catching their breaths. As Dani finally came off the sex-infused high, she couldn't believe she'd allowed it to happen again.

"Dylan." She tapped him on the shoulder.

"Right, sorry." He pulled out of her and rolled onto his back.

Dani turned onto her side, facing him. She tucked her hands under her pillow as she lay there staring at the rock god, both of them not saying a word. What was going through Dylan's mind? She knew what was going through hers. They were being irresponsible. She didn't want to end up pregnant. Neither one of them needed that stress in their lives. She needed to put a stop to it.

Besides, she didn't know where she stood with Dylan. He wasn't a relationship kind of guy. So what did that make her?

"I've been thinking." Dylan broke the silence.

"Me too." She squeezed her pillow tight. Did she really want to do this? Was she ready to walk away?

"You first."

Dani swallowed hard and gathered up the courage to spill her guts. "I really care about you, Dylan."

"I care about you too, cupcake." He reached over and tenderly tucked her hair behind her ear. Her heart broke. "I can't deny it."

"I feel like I've made a big mistake coming here." A tear rolled down her cheek. "I thought I could separate my feelings for you and work, but here I am jealous of your ex and thinking of ways to be in your life."

"Since we're being honest, I totally wanted to kill Benny Boy last night." Dylan rolled over and faced her. "You know when we were talking about things we can and can't control?"

Dani nodded.

"I can't control my feelings for you, and I've accepted that I can't change that."

"So, what are those feelings?"

Dylan exhaled a shaky breath. "There's not another woman out there I want to fuck."

"Um. I don't think that's a feeling, but thanks. I think."

"Fuck, that didn't come out right."

"Try again."

"All I know is my life is much brighter with you in it." He caressed her cheek. "I think about you all time."

Dani grinned, biting her bottom lip. "Really?"

"I guess what I'm trying to say is I want you in my life on a deeper level, Dani Clark." Dani gazed deep into his blue-gray eyes, speechless.

"You're quiet for someone who always has a lot to say."

Dani didn't know what to think. Singing straight to her heart, he'd said everything she'd longed to hear. She wanted their relationship, or whatever it was, to be more than just sex. Did she dare to believe in happily ever after with a rock star? She knew better than to let her guard down, but as she gazed deeply into his eyes, Dani couldn't walk away either, even though she knew this man would destroy her heart.

"Dani, I get it if you want to leave. I'm not the easiest person to love."

Dani cupped his face and kissed him. "I don't want to leave, but I don't want to be your fix either."

"Having sex with you was never a drug for me. I see you now that I'm sober."

Was this the change she'd been looking for? If so, why wasn't she convinced?

Her guard was still up. She wanted to believe him and have her happily ever after, but she wasn't easily fooled. Dylan was sober, and that was amazing, but he still had demons.

"So, you want to do this thing?"

Dani knew she couldn't nor shouldn't press his childhood issues. She needed to be more patient. He'd tell her. A wide smile spread across her lips, and she nodded.

"Yeah?"

"Let's take it slow, okay?" She'd fantasized about the day Dylan would want to take their friendship to another level. And each fantasy ended in heartache. But this was different because Dylan was sober.

"Slow is something I'm not used to, cupcake. But for you I'd be willing to try."

Dani leaned in and kissed him sweetly. "As long as you try, I'm good with that. I do have one condition."

"Anything, cupcake."

"No more unprotected sex. And that we're exclusive."

"Fuck, I'm sorry."

"It's not *totally* your fault. I could have stopped it."

Dylan flashed her a devious grin. "No, you can't. You can't deny a rock god."

Dani rolled her eyes. "God, help me."

"Well, I don't know about that, but I can help you out of this T-shirt." He tugged the bottom of her shirt. "We need to seal the deal with naked cuddles."

Before she knew it, her shirt was on the floor, and her body was pressed against a wall of lean tattooed muscle. She snuggled in close.

Every day was a whirlwind with Dylan Grace. She never knew what to expect. It was what kept her on her toes. However, Dani had seen growth in Dylan's wellbeing and their relationship. They were both growing and moving beyond casual sex. Together, they could do this.

God, please don't let me be wrong.

15

*G*racefall gathered in the control room, listening to the playback on the last track for their new album. Dylan hovered over Alex, their music producer, and Butch, their sound technician. He couldn't believe it; they had pulled off the impossible. In two months, working around the clock, Gracefall had gelled together unlike any time before and produced their best heavy metal album to date. It was gritty, it was raw, it was rock and roll.

As they played back the songs, Dylan had been shocked at the realness of his lyrics. Collaborating with his brother again felt damn good. They were fucking amazing together. Even the couple of songs that Jake had written were brilliant.

Dylan couldn't remember a time when he felt this way about Gracefall. The band had been through hell since making it. Between losing Moxie and Dylan's overdose almost destroying the band, the guys deserved some good news. This album was it. A new beginning in more ways than one for him.

The track ended and silence filled the room. Dylan

turned to his bandmates. Joe stood with his arms crossed, stone-faced and unreadable as usual. Tyler was sitting on the edge of the couch, resting his forearms on his thighs, staring at the floor. Jake stood staring at the soundboard, stroking his goatee, while Elliot rocked back and forth nervously on her heels, waiting for someone to say something.

Fuck, Dylan wished he knew what they thought because he felt these songs were kick-ass, balls to the wall, the next level of Gracefall at its best.

Dylan couldn't hold the excitement back any longer. "Fuck yeah, dude!"

"I'm blown away. Speechless," Jake said.

"That's a first," Elliot teased. "Seriously, I've never played like this before. Babe." She turned to Jake. "We sound amazing together. And Dylan, your vocals are spot on."

Dylan couldn't wipe the shit-eating grin from his face. Hell yeah, Gracefall was back.

Tyler stood and walked over to Dylan with open arms and a tear in his eye. "That was fucking beautiful, bro." He hugged Dylan, squeezing the air out of his lungs.

"T, I can't breathe."

Tyler let up and took a step back as he wiped his eyes. "What say you, Joe?"

Everyone looked at Joe. He was still standing with his arms crossed and staring at the control panel. They all waited for him to say something. Sweat rolled down Dylan's spine in anticipation. Fuck, he hoped he'd met his brother's expectations.

"God damn," Joe murmured. "Two months, and we've given birth to a beast."

Dylan couldn't contain himself. He strode over to his brother and hugged him.

"This is the best fucking Gracefall record we've ever recorded." Joe pounded his fist against Dylan's back. "Never been prouder of you, little bro."

It felt good, damn good, being back in Joe's good graces. It felt even better pleasing him and his bandmates.

Dylan was not dissing all he'd accomplished either. He was damn proud he was finding his way again, not only with the band but also with his recovery. And a big part of that was thanks to Dani—she believed in him, and that was something.

Dylan released his hold on Joe. His brother faced the rest of the band. "Never been prouder of all of you."

Gracefall lit up the room, celebrating their success, and all Dylan could think of was sharing this moment with Dani. "Let's call the girls in and let them listen to the new material."

"I'll text Cherry," Tyler said as he pulled out his phone. "I'm sure she and Tomi would be interested."

"Yep, Mel should be here," Joe added, following Tyler's lead.

"I can't wait for Dani to hear this." Fast as his fingers could type, Dylan sent off a text to Dani. He looked up to find everyone staring at him. "What?"

"It's about fucking time you made her your girlfriend." Tyler slapped his shoulder. "If you'd waited much longer, I would have made a move." A shy grin crept across his mouth.

"First of all," Dylan began, quite annoyed at the mental picture of Tyler and Dani together looping in his brain, "Dani is not my girlfriend."

"Right," Joe added as he texted.

Dylan ignored him as he went on. "And second, over my dead body."

"If Dani's not your girlfriend," Elliot jumped in, apparently striking a nerve, "then she can date whoever she wants."

"I never said she could date other people."

"Don't be a dick," Elliot said. "Don't keep her hanging on. All I'm saying is if you like her, and it's pretty apparent that you do, make her your girlfriend. Give her something she can count on."

"I give her plenty to count on." Dylan grabbed his dick. Seriously, what was with Elliot the Buzzkill?

Elliot rolled her eyes.

"Everything is perfect between Dani and me as is. We have an understanding."

"Fine." Elliot raised her hands, done with the conversation.

Everything was indeed perfect. Gracefall was back, he was sober, and he had Dani. The rock god had returned.

~

*D*ani sat at the kitchen island scrolling through her classes on her laptop. She cringed as she viewed her grades for the quarter. She'd never failed a class in her life, let alone three easy online classes she should have been able to handle. She didn't even look to see if she'd missed the deadline for fall enrollment, not with these grades.

Melody had been right; Dylan was a full-time job.

The last two months had been a rock and roll roller coaster of crazy. Dylan was killing it on his sobriety and even finding time for meditation, which was the only way she could get him to talk. He was still guarded, only letting her know what he wanted her to know. And relationship talk was definitely off the table. He had been super focused on the band and their new album. There'd been a few days where Dylan had spent the whole day and then some in the studio without breaking. It had concerned her that he might have been working too hard, so she spent time in the studio with him, making sure he was handling everything the best he could.

There had been a party or two and a gig here and there, which were always a blast. Keeping up with a rock star hadn't been easy, and somewhere along the way Dani had lost herself. She was right back to feeling like she was Dylan's fuck buddy. They would hang out, which would lead to sex, which would then lead to Dylan leaving after. No cuddles. No waking up in his arms feeling loved. She felt alone, even when he was sitting next her, and she didn't know how to fix it when Dylan didn't want to talk about it.

Thinking about how she'd spent the last few days, Dani had to ask the question: Why was she here?

Gracefall had finished laying down the tracks on their new album, they were gearing up to promote a new single, and they were heading back to LA for production rehearsals for upcoming shows. Soon, tour announcements would be made, band interviews would be booked, and everyone would want a piece of Dylan Grace.

Where would she fit in?

Dylan had promised he'd make things work between them, but a couple naked cooking sessions hadn't done the trick; they'd always led to sex. And the sex was amazing, but Dani needed more. She needed to wake up in the morning with Dylan's arms wrapped around her. At this point she'd even take him staying in bed with her instead of leaving in the middle of the night. She wanted to be introduced as his girlfriend, not just by her name. She didn't want to be shot down every time she brought up the future.

She wanted a relationship—a relationship he didn't want.

Dani huffed in defeat as she rested her head in her hands. What was she going to do? There was no doubt Dylan cared for her; he showed her in his Dylan ways, but with his life revving into overdrive, Dani couldn't see this "thing" they had working, and it broke her heart.

Dani closed her laptop and pulled out her cellphone. She scrolled through her contacts and stopped at her parents' numbers. She missed her mom and dad and friends back in LA. Six months was a long time to be away from family and definitely enough time for Dylan to sort out his feelings for her. Dani called her mom, and it went straight to voicemail. She didn't bother leaving a message.

"Hey." Melody walked in and instantly read Dani's mood. "What's wrong?"

Dani shrugged. "Everything."

"This is not like you. Talk to me." Melody sat down on the barstool next to Dani.

Tears threatened to well in Dani's eyes, but she pushed forward. "I failed my online classes."

"What?"

"I know." Dani slouched, feeling like a complete failure. "I couldn't keep up."

Her friend said nothing, obviously still in shock.

"I don't even know what I'm doing anymore." Dani hid her face in her hands. Why was she so damn emotional? She could fix this. She knew what she needed to do, but her heart wouldn't let go.

"I think it's time that you go back to LA."

Dani was silent.

"Get back to the ordinary world?"

Dani nodded.

"I completely understand. Living the rock and roll life isn't for the faint of heart."

"Yeah, but you have Joe to help you navigate through it. I don't even know where I stand with Dylan. I get the whole no relationship thing, but I need more."

"Have you talked to him?"

"I try." Dani fidgeted with the corner of her laptop. "Whenever I bring up the future, he shuts down. I mean, I know he cares."

"I know you're right. From my conversations with Joe, he's never seen Dylan this committed to one woman. You've done a lot for him, and you're the reason that his sobriety has been a success."

"Yeah, I'm pretty proud of him." The corner of her mouth raised a little. "But, Mel, I need my life back. I'm behind a semester in school."

"Dani, seriously, we need to fix that."

"I know." Dani sat back and sighed. "I don't know what to do. I'm so confused. I want to stay and be with Dylan, but I know staying will only prolong the inevitable that Dylan doesn't want me as his girlfriend. Besides, Mel, you should see how he looks at Ash. I wouldn't be surprised if they end up back together."

"Ash over you? No way. Trust me on that one." Melody reached over and held Dani's arm. "If you want to go back home, I can totally make that happen. I'll cash in a couple of my being engaged to a rock star perks. Have you ever been on Gracefall's private jet?"

Dani shook her head.

"Oh, you're in for a treat."

The best friends shared a smile.

"If you're serious about going back to LA, I'll go with you. We have two months until the wedding. Lots to do."

"Two months?"

Melody nodded.

Dani's phone buzzed exactly at the same time Melody's did. They both read the text messages, then looked at each other with huge smiles on their faces.

A while later, Dani looked at Dylan after the last track was played. Gracefall's new album had left her speechless. She'd never heard the band gel together like this before. It was so good she got goosebumps.

He was a musical poet, and when he sang his voice transcended through your soul—not too much different than the Dylan of past, but clearer, more connected and emotional. Definitely a head-banger album but beyond that. Dani almost felt like crying because this was pure evidence he was on his way to being well, and she was so happy for him.

"I know, right?" Dylan was looking at her with a beaming smile on his face.

"Dylan, this is amazing." She rushed over, giving him a hug. "I'm so proud of you. Just look at how far you've come."

He picked her up and twirled her around. "I've never been so happy. I can't believe we recorded a kick-ass album in two months." He put her down. "I can't wait to get back to LA. Big Rick will shit when he hears this album."

"I'm sure he will," Dani agreed.

"Kimmy better be ready to promote the hell out of it."

As Dylan went on about everything that needed to be done, Dani became depressed. Her time with Dylan was up. The agreement was she'd be Dylan's life coach until the album was done. Now that it was finished, everything was about to change. When they returned to LA, where would she fit into his life? She feared they would go back to being fuck buddies, and there was no way she'd revert to that. That was her past, not her future. Her heart couldn't take the pain of Dylan Grace coming in and out of her life whenever he needed her. She had needs, too, like wanting to be a special part of his life. Not someone who was just there to fill a void. So, where did that leave her?

She pondered the question and quickly concluded. It was time she woke up from this rock star dream and accepted reality.

The chemistry between them was hot and passionate, and the sex was mind-blowing. The man was extraordinarily talented with his tongue, and his bedroom vocabulary would make the devil himself blush. Everything was perfect until she woke in the morning without Dylan lying next to her. Dani didn't understand why he'd leave after she fell asleep. He was still harboring inner demons that she knew nothing about.

Everything seemed to be a distraction from what was really going on. There were times Dylan was far way, out of reach, and that scared her. She'd tried to get him to open up, but it either ended up in a fight or with Dylan deflecting the issue to something else.

The thought of going back to LA, back to Dylan's past, worried her.

"When are you leaving for LA?"

"End of the week."

Nausea rolled in her stomach. Five days was all she had left. She waited for Dylan to say something, anything to make her change her mind about their situation, but he said nothing, and she wasn't going to bring it up and ruin the time they had left together. To be honest, she didn't want to hear it. She already knew.

Dani wrapped her arms around his neck, loving the way he gripped her hips, pulling her close. "How are we celebrating?"

"I think Cherry said she was booking the VIP room at the club we played a while back. Something small. The big party will be in LA."

Oh good, another reminder.

Dylan's mood turned serious as he framed her face with his soft hands. "I couldn't have done this without you. You know that, right?"

Dani swallowed past the lump forming in her throat. "You deserve all the credit. You made it happen. I was just there to coach you along."

Dylan shook his head. "Stop being so humble and learn how to take a compliment. You're the rock star."

Dani blushed and avoided his gaze as the compliment made her feel awkward. She hated it when he was right.

Dani's knees threatened to buckle as Dylan pulled her back under his smoldering stare. "You're *my* fucking rock star."

Speechless, Dani melted right there in Dylan's arms as he kissed her. She felt weightless as his tongue danced with hers, as their bodies crashed together, as she dared to believe him.

The kiss broke, and she rested her forehead against his, catching her breath. The urge to tell him that she loved him sat heavily at the tip of her tongue, itching to be said. She stomped out that thought quickly. Confessing her love would have had the rocker running to the hills. No, she'd stay right here, savoring the moment when Dylan Grace had called her his.

16

"*F*uck, that was amazing." Dylan rolled over, breathless.

Dani pulled her bedsheet up to cover her naked, beautifully aching body and lay back down. After celebrating all night into the early morning, Dani's head still thumped from the music at the club.

"We are so good at that." The weight of the mattress lifted as Dylan got up and headed to the bathroom. She heard the toilet flush and the faucet run.

Dylan was right. The only thing solid between them was the mind-blowing sex. Emotionally he wasn't there. Not like he should be, and she hated waking up alone. Something had to change, but she didn't know if she was ready for that reality.

Dylan returned wearing a pair of jeans. Dani sat up. "Are you leaving?"

"Yeah." He rubbed the back of his neck. Obviously, something had been bothering him.

"You don't have to go." Dani's heart raced. "I'd like it if you'd stay."

Dylan exhaled heavily as he sat on the edge of the bed. "Dani, I'm not going there with you."

"Why? I don't understand. What does spending the night in bed together and waking up together in the morning matter?"

"We have a good thing going. Let's not complicate it."

The way he brushed her off made her angry. He wasn't going to get away with this. "So, it's good that I feel like your fuck buddy rather than your girlfriend?"

Dylan squeezed his eyes shut, clearly annoyed at her. "How long have you known me? I don't do relationships."

"Then what am I to you? You said that you wanted me in your life on a deeper level, but nothing has changed."

Dylan flopped back onto the bed, his tattooed arm draped over his eyes. "Look, I'm trying."

"It's not good enough. You're holding something back that's hurting both of us." Dani had to do something; he had to know that she was serious.

"What do you want, Dani?"

"I want all of you. I want to feel loved, not used."

Dylan sat up, angry. "You think I'm using you?"

"Nothing's changed, has it? I'm no more to you than I was before."

Dylan stood and faced her. He looked as though he was searching for the right words to say. Instead of talking, he walked toward the door.

Dani scrambled out of bed, taking the bedsheet with her. "Wait. You don't get to leave."

Dylan strode out of the room before she could stop him. "Dylan, stop. Let's talk about this."

His bedroom door slammed shut, then she heard Metallica blaring.

Tears streamed down her face. What had just

happened? Bile rose into her throat. Quickly, she headed to the bathroom in time to make it to the toilet, where she violently puked twice.

After heaving for the last time, Dani sat back on her heels. Her eyes widened, and she laid her hand on her stomach. "Oh no."

After a couple of minutes sitting on the cold hardwood floor, Dani came to. She couldn't be pregnant; she had a period last month, although it was light, and she was on the pill.

Dani stood on weak legs as she washed her face, welcoming the cold water cooling her heated skin, then she rinsed her mouth. Eyeing a black T-shirt flung over the jacuzzi tub, she put it on and walked into her bedroom to grab a pair of underwear. What she wouldn't do for a cold glass of water.

After dressing, Dani made her way downstairs to the kitchen. On her way, she couldn't shake the thought of being pregnant. Unfortunately, the closest convenience store wasn't so convenient since it was forty minutes away. She could wait until she arrived in LA to take a pregnancy test. Until then, she had to keep her shit together.

Dani grabbed a glass and filled it with ice cubes and water. She sipped it until she felt the nausea go away. Yeah, she wasn't pregnant. It was nerves. She hated fighting with Dylan, and she had been super nervous about bringing up their relationship, but it had to be done.

Dani leaned against the counter. God, she hated herself for loving a man who didn't love her back.

The front door opened, startling her. It was probably Mac doing a walkthrough.

"Hey." Ash walked into the kitchen.

Dani looked at the clock. Was it really five o'clock in the morning? "Hey."

"Is Dylan awake? I need to talk to him."

Dani shrugged. "It's five a.m. He's probably sleeping." She knew damn well he wasn't sleeping, but she wasn't about to send the redhead to his room. Especially after their fight. "I'm not his keeper."

"What's your problem with me?" Ash folded her arms across her chest. "What have I done to you?"

"Oh, I don't know. Maybe it has everything to do with Dylan."

"Look, we're just friends."

Dani nodded. "Right. I'm not stupid. I see the way you look at him. You still love him."

Ash looked away as if Dani had hit the nail on the head.

"Oh my God, it's true." Dani's biggest fear was manifesting right in front of her.

"Listen, Dylan will always hold a special place in my heart. But we're completely over." Ash took in her outfit. "He never shared his rock concert tees with me."

There was so much Dani wanted to air out, like all the times she had been there for Dylan when Ash had screwed him over. Seriously, dating Davidson was a low blow, and she flaunted it right in front of his face.

"You know what?" Dani placed her glass in the sink. "I'm not going there with you."

"Hey," Dylan walked into the kitchen. "I thought I heard voices down here. What's going on?"

"Nothing." Dani pushed past him. "She wants to talk to you."

∾

"Trouble in paradise?" Ash smirked.

"Fuck off." Dylan turned around to head back upstairs. Fighting with one woman was enough. He didn't need Ash on his ass too.

"Dylan, wait. We need to talk."

Dylan studied Ash's face; she had been crying. Something was seriously wrong. "What's going on, Ash?"

Ash threw a stack of papers on the counter. "I found this on Davidson's desk."

Suspiciously, he took the stack of papers and flipped through the documents. "What am I looking for?"

"These are my band's bank statements. The statements on the bottom are from Gracefall's account." She pointed to a specific withdrawal. "Look at how many times he's made withdrawals under the name 'Road Cash.' I highlighted them all."

"There's a lot to pay out on the road. I'm sure there's nothing to worry about." Dylan scanned the statement. "Shit, there's at least twenty thousand dollars withdrawn on the first page?"

"I know. Now, look at your account."

Dylan flipped through the stack and found Gracefall's account. The same withdrawals stared right back at him. "Holy fucking shit!"

"If my math is right, an easy fifty thousand was withdrawn."

Dylan fell right into denial because he could believe his manager would steal from the band. "Maybe this is legit. I mean, our tour production has tripled in size. Everyone has to get paid. Did you confront Davidson about this?"

"I did and got a lame ass excuse."

"What did he say?"

Ash shrugged. "He said road cash was for paying expenses on the road. And I understand that, but when I asked for a detailed breakdown of payments, he got really defensive. That's when I went digging further and found an account tied to a business I'd never heard of. I can't find it anywhere on the internet. Dylan, there are thousands in that account, more than both of our accounts combined. That bastard is stealing from us."

"Wait, that's a huge allegation. Even though I hate the asshole, he's been with the band since the beginning."

"I know, but Gracefall has taken off, and he's capitalizing on that. He's stealing your hard-earned money. Besides, he's been hanging around this one guy who gives me the creeps. He might be part of the whole scheme."

Dylan looked back at the statements; thousands of dollars missing. There was no way his roadies made more than him.

"I'm hiring a private attorney that's not associated with the record company to do a full audit on my accounts. I highly suggest you do the same."

He couldn't believe this was happening right under his nose. Then again, he'd been too fucked up to notice or even care, but that didn't mean the other band members had to suffer. The bastard had taken Ash and money from him.

"Fucking Davidson." Dylan shook his head.

"I'm sorry." He felt Ash's hand on his shoulder. "I'm sorry for ever leaving you for him."

Dylan squeezed his eyes shut. They weren't slipping back into the past. He was finally free from Ash and their toxic relationship.

"I should have been more patient with you."

"No, Ash." Dylan opened his eyes and saw the hurt in hers. At one time, he'd loved the beautiful redhead. He'd fallen fast and loved hard, which always ended with him hurting someone he cared about. No matter how hard he tried to change his fate, Dylan Grace was born to self-destruct. It wasn't fair to bring her or anyone else along for the ride. "You weren't to blame. I pushed you away. I was too fucked up to appreciate what I had." And didn't that insight hit him hard as he thought of Dani? She had been right. He needed to give more.

"I appreciate your honesty." She smiled. "I like the new Dylan Grace."

Dylan rubbed the back of his neck. Certainly being off the drugs had given him better perspective and clarity. "Yeah, I'm a work in progress. At least, that's what Dani says."

"She's right. You should listen to her. She's good for you."

Dylan shook his head. "She's too good."

Not wanting to regress, Dylan took in a deep breath and pushed on. He was done visiting darkness. "Can I have these?" He lifted the stack of papers.

"Yeah, I made copies."

"I'll show Joe and see what he wants to do."

"That's a good first step."

"So, what are you going to do?"

"I'm flying back to LA in the morning, alone. I don't ever want to see Davidson's face again."

"Seems like that's where everyone is heading."

"Home sweet home." They shared a smile.

17

*I*t was midafternoon, and Dani lay on the couch in her beachside Santa Monica apartment. She was still wearing her bathrobe and feeling horrible from a stomach bug she'd been suffering from since being back home. Two weeks had passed, and she was no closer to purging her thoughts of Dylan Grace. Food, on the other hand, was a different story. Dani knew mending her broken heart would be difficult but being sick added another layer of misery. No amount of rocky road ice cream was going to save her.

Just thinking of ice cream made her stomach churn.

Too weak to get off the couch, Dani rolled over, facing the bucket Melody had brought her for this very reason. Dani closed her eyes, praying she'd do anything for the vomiting to stop. Breathing through nausea, she dozed off.

"Dani." She heard Melody's voice but couldn't move. "Dani." She felt her body shake as she slowly opened her eyes.

Melody kneeled down in front of her. "How are you feeling?"

"Horrible," Dani muttered as she sat up.

"I brought you some Gatorade and chicken noodle soup."

"Thanks." Dani fidgeted on the couch, trying to get comfortable as she felt Melody studying her. "What?"

"Did you, you know?"

"Know what?"

Melody rolled her eyes. "Take the pregnancy test I bought you?"

"Yes."

"And?"

"No, I'm not pregnant. I have the flu, Mel."

Melody got up and walked into the kitchen. "You haven't been able to keep anything down for almost two weeks. I think it's time you saw your doctor."

"I'll be fine." Dani stood slowly, not telling Melody that she was dizzy as hell. It would pass.

"I'd feel better if you'd go and at least get checked out. You'd feel better."

Dani heard the microwave running as she made her way to her dining room table, where a cold Gatorade was waiting for her. Thank God she had a best friend like Melody checking in on her. "Hey, I really appreciate you taking the time to stop by. I know the wedding is right around the corner. I feel bad not being there for you."

"First of all, that's what friends are for." Melody set a bowl of soup in front of her then sat down. "Second, your health is much more important than my wedding. We need to get you well. You're not missing the wedding of the year," Melody joked.

"I wouldn't miss it for the world." Dani picked up her spoon. Fighting past nausea, she forced herself to take a sip. The warmth of the soup made her feel better and was definitely an improvement from the crackers she'd been eating.

"Dylan is back in town."

Hearing his name made her pause. Made her want to pick up her cell and call him, but she refused. "That's nice." Dani continued to take another sip.

"I take it he hasn't called you?"

"No." And she didn't expect a call, not after the fight they'd had back in Tennessee. The flight back to LA kept looping in her memories. Dylan wouldn't look at her. When they had landed, he'd raced off the jet without saying good-bye, then hopped into the limo waiting for him.

Just like that, Dani was out of his life.

Dani looked up from her soup. Melody's lips were pressed together as if she was holding her tongue.

"Go ahead. Tell me I told you so. Tell me I'm a fool for thinking I could keep my heart safe from Dylan Grace." Melody didn't say a word. She didn't need to; it was written all over her face. "I'll be fine."

"I know you will. You guys will work things out."

"I don't think so. He hasn't called me once."

"I wouldn't give up yet."

Dani looked at Melody, confused. "Whose side are you on?"

"Yours, of course."

"Great. I don't want to hear Dylan's name ever again. In fact, I don't ever want to see him again."

"Umm, that might be a problem. You're my maid of honor, and Dylan is Joe's best man."

"Well, fine. After the wedding, I don't ever want to see Dylan again."

"Okay." Melody shook her head.

"What, you don't believe me?"

"No, no, I believe you." Melody gave Dani a knowing smile.

"Just stop. I don't want to talk about him." Dani stood too fast, and the room spun. Her knees buckled.

"Dani!" Melody shot out of the chair and caught Dani before she hit the floor.

"I think we should go to the ER."

"I think you're right," Melody agreed.

Before Dani knew what was happening, she was in Melody's car, racing to the emergency room.

18

"*S*low the fuck down!"

Dylan smirked at Joe sitting in the passenger seat, white-knuckling the "oh shit" bar in his Aston Martin DBS Superleggera as he took a sharp right down a blacktop road through Death Valley.

"Live fast, die young, bro." Dylan switched gears and punched it.

"I'd like to live, fuck you very much." Dylan laughed at the sight of Joe's big, fidgety body crammed into the passenger seat, white as a ghost.

"Don't worry. We're almost there."

"Thank fuck. Next time, I'm driving."

Dylan slowed as he reached the hidden turnoff onto the outskirts of the desert. As the valley opened, he saw he was in the right place. "We're here."

He parked, and Joe hopped out of the car. "She's hell on wheels." Joe patted the hood.

Dylan shut the car door. "Fuck yeah, dude. Love at first sight." The first week he'd been back in LA, he'd gone car shopping and house hunting. For the first time in his life, he'd felt like laying down roots.

He'd hooked back up with the clinic's psychiatrist and discussed more of what was holding him back. Yep, he'd divulged some of the most detailed, intimate shit he'd ever shared with anyone. Dylan was determined to win and get his girl.

Dylan led them to a massive rock formation and climbed on top. Joe followed. The brothers stood looking out into the valley.

Surprise came over Joe's face. "Is that our trailer?"

"Yep," Dylan answered with a huge smile on his lips as he gazed out several feet away at his childhood home. He looked down at his watch; they were right on time. "Keep watching."

"Dylan, what the fuck is going on? I'm in no mood for your bullshit," Joe grumbled.

"You'll like this bullshit. Trust me. Shut up and keep watching." Dylan pulled out two cigars and handed one to his brother.

Joe examined the smoke. "What's this for?"

Dylan lit his cigar and inhaled a long, deep drag. "Trust me." He handed Joe the lighter. "It will make it that much sweeter."

Dylan stood and posed like a rocker on stage. He belted out a five-count countdown. "Five, four, three, two, one!" Right before his eyes, their childhood nightmare exploded into millions of pieces. "Fuck yeah, dude."

As the flames burned the trailer to ash, Dylan looked over at Joe, who slowly removed his hands from his ears, completely shocked. "What the?"

"I can't tell you how many times I've wished that fucker would go up in flames."

"How in the hell?" Joe's mouth was wide open.

Dylan sat down, followed by Joe, and took a drag from his cigar. "I paid a house moving company to remove the piece of shit and bring it out here to the desert, then I paid our pyrotechnic crew to blow it up." Dylan turned to Joe. "Don't worry, I got a permit, sort of. I don't know if it's totally legal, but—" Dylan shrugged.

"Tyler would be proud, bro."

They looked out over the mass of burning trash, smoldering in plumes of gray and black smoke. Dylan had never experienced peace like this before. It was as if his past was erased entirely. At least this part of it.

"Part of the twelve-step program is asking for forgiveness from those you've hurt. Bro, I know I hurt you."

"You did." Joe stared into the flames. "Your drug use was like a slap in the face. I did everything in my power to keep you safe, and I failed."

"You didn't fail. I fucked up. And I want to say I'm sorry."

Joe breathed in deeply. "Well, watching our past go up in smoke feels fucking good." Joe smiled at Dylan.

"Yeah, it does."

"You're forgiven, little bro."

Joe's words were like a soothing salve over his soul. He hadn't realized, until now, how much he'd needed his brother's forgiveness. If only he could forgive himself. That was next.

"I know I don't say it as much as I should, but I'm proud of you. You've taken your sobriety seriously, and that makes me happy for you and the band. It takes a lot of courage to do what you're doing. It's not easy, especially dealing with the abuse from your past, of which I still don't really know the whole of. I wish..." His brother's voice cracked, and he couldn't say anymore. Dylan knew where Joe was going, and it broke his heart.

"Don't. It was unfair to put that kind of responsibility on a thirteen-year-old kid. You did the best you could. I would have been far worse if you hadn't been there. I remember the night you put Mom's boyfriend in the hospital for beating the shit out of me. I remember thinking how cool it was that my big brother was a hero."

Joe wiped his eyes. "Aw, fuck."

Dylan looked at the burning trailer and lay back, resting the weight of his body on his arms. "Fucking beautiful day. Can't keep us Grace boys down for long."

Silence fell between them as they watched the trailer turn to ash. For once in Dylan's life, he felt at peace. *Ding, dong, the wicked witch is dead.*

"So, what do you think Karen will do when she returns to find her home gone?" Joe puffed on his cigar. "Not that I care."

"I took care of Mom."

"You found her?"

"It wasn't hard. I tracked her down at a crack house. I cleaned her up, put her ass on a plane to Florida, and checked her into an extensive drug rehab center."

"You're a better man than me."

"Joe, hate keeps us prisoners. You know how to break free?"

Joe didn't say a word.

"Love."

"Sobriety has turned you into a pussy," Joe teased.

Dylan laughed. It felt amazing being free.

Joe's cellphone rang, and he answered. "Hey, babe. What's up? What?" The tone in Joe's voice worried Dylan. Something was wrong. "Is she okay?"

Dylan sat up and turned to Joe. "Who?"

Joe held up his hand to hush him. "Yeah, he's here. We'll be right there." Joe hung up and looked at Dylan. A grimness spread across his face. "Dani's in the hospital."

"What!"

"I don't know all the details. Mel said they are waiting to see a doctor."

"Fuck!" Dylan stood. "We gotta go." He climbed off the rock in record speed and strode back to the car with Joe right behind him.

"I'm driving," Joe said, holding his hand out, waiting for the car keys.

"The fuck you are. You drive like a grandma."

"At least we'll get there safely. Now hand it over."

"Fine." Dylan tossed the keys to Joe. "You better get us there before I lose my shit."

The brothers got into the car and pulled out onto the road heading to the hospital. Dylan's heart raced a mile a minute. Dani had to be all right. Being out in no man's land, they were at least an hour or more away before they reached the city. *Fuck!*

"Punch it, dude!" Dylan yelled. "I swear to fuck!"

"Calm down. Mel is with Dani, and they are at the hospital. Everything will be fine."

Dylan had never been so scared in his life. He didn't know if he believed in God. In his experience, God had forgotten about him, but he prayed anyway, hoping that just one time, He would hear his plea to keep Dani safe.

Dylan rushed into the ER and checked in. Once cleared, he made a mad dash to the waiting room, where he met Melody. "Mellie, where's Dani? Is she okay?" Dylan asked, out of breath.

"They just took her back."

"What happened?"

"She passed out. Dani's been fighting the stomach flu for the last two weeks, but you'd know that if you had called her." Melody glared at him. "And it didn't help that she was strung out over you."

"Mellie—"

"Don't Mellie me. You fucked up."

Shit, Mel was using her mom voice. He was fucked.

Melody's face wrinkled in anger. "Dani gave up everything for you. Did you know she had one more semester until she graduated? You need to get your head out of your ass and do right by Dani. If not, you need to get out of her life for good."

What? Had Dani given up her career to be his life coach? "Mel, I thought she was taking online classes. I would never ask her to give up anything."

"You didn't ask her. It's always about you."

Joe walked into the room. *Perfect timing.* Mellie was hitting hard.

"Well, looks like you guys are getting along." Joe hugged Melody, kissing her forehead.

"I just can't anymore." Melody walked to the back of the waiting room to the coffee station.

Dylan exhaled. Mel was right; he'd messed up. He hated knowing that he'd made Dani feel like she was being used, and worse yet she'd dropped out of school. But that was what he did; he used people. His relationship with Dani had been purely sexual until he'd gotten clean. Now, after spending time with her, it scared him that he could see himself settling down.

The last two weeks had been spent figuring his shit out. He missed Dani. He'd bought a house, thinking that starting anew would help, but every time he'd walked into a room, it had felt empty, cold. All he could think about was Dani, and he'd found himself planning out a room for her to meditate and study in. Fuck, he needed to make that right.

He'd bought a sportscar thinking he needed a fast, new woman in his life. Again, he'd found himself on a joyride, looking at the passenger side, imagining how incredibly sexy Dani would look smiling back at him with the wind blowing through her hair.

He'd missed her warm smile, her signature red lipstick, even her positivity. But was it fair to bring her into his life of chaos and darkness? He had already hurt her.

Dylan was working through his demons. The trailer and settling his mom were two of them. There were still more to tackle. He thought if he worked through them, he'd be ready to give himself to Dani, but maybe he was wrong. Maybe the day would never come. Why did he have to be so fucked up?

The doctor walked into the room, grabbing everyone's attention. "Miss Stirling?"

"Yes." Melody walked over to the doctor. "How is she?"

"Your friend is fine. She's very dehydrated."

"Can I see her?" Dylan asked.

The doctor looked at Melody, and she nodded. "She's resting, but yes, Miss Clark can have visitors."

Dylan pushed past the doctor and strode past the nurses' station, getting starry-eyed glances. If he were anyone else, they would have stopped him.

He came to the end of the hall. The curtain to the room was halfway open. Cautiously, he peeked inside. His heart sank. Dani was asleep in a hospital bed hooked up to an IV. As he gazed at her, something came over him, hitting him like a ton a lead. He couldn't live without this woman in his life.

Quietly, he stepped inside the room, pulling the curtain closed. He wheeled the doctor's stool over to Dani's bedside and sat down. Dylan rubbed his sweaty hands down his jean-covered thighs. Her long dark hair was spread out behind her on the pillow, her skin was pale. He took her hand in his, caressing the back of it with his thumb.

"I'm sorry I didn't call," he whispered, not wanting to wake her. "I should have never let you walk away." He brought her hand to his mouth. He closed his eyes as he brushed his lips against her skin. "I'm a fucking dumbass."

"Well, that's one thing we can agree on."

Dylan opened his eyes. Her vibrant blue eyes warmed his heart...among other body parts. "Did I wake you?"

Dani pulled her hand away. "What are you doing here?" She sat up.

"Here, let me help." Dylan took the bed remote, set the recline control, and then fluffed her pillows. "There."

Dani lay back.

"Comfy?"

She nodded.

Silence fell between them as Dylan sensed something was on Dani's mind by the way she avoided eye contact and fidgeted with the hem of the bedsheet. "I should have called you."

Dani shook her head.

"I thought about you every day."

Her gaze snapped to his; tears filled her eyes. The silent treatment was killing him.

"If it makes things better, I'll bend over and you can kick my ass."

"Dylan, I don't want to kick your ass." Dylan exhaled finally. She was talking. "There are times I want to choke you."

"Like now?"

"Yeah, like now. Dylan, I'm pregnant."

Dylan's gaze slowly met Dani's. *What the?* "Pregnant?" He swallowed hard.

"Yes."

"Like there's a bun in the oven?"

Dani nodded.

"Holy fuck, cupcake." Shocked to the core, Dylan stood up and shoved his hand through his hair. He went numb with the thought of being a father. "You told me you were on the pill."

"If you are suggesting I lied, you can leave right now."

"No, that's not what I'm saying."

"The doctor ran a pregnancy test. I guess my home test was faulty. I seriously thought I had the stomach flu."

"A baby? A fucking baby?" No matter how many times he said it, he couldn't believe it.

"Listen, Dylan, I'm just as shocked as you."

"Knock, knock." The doctor walked in.

Great timing, doc.

"How are you feeling?" The good doctor walked over and checked the IV bag.

"Much better."

"Good." He sat down on the stool Dylan had been sitting on and reviewed his notes. "Your numbers look good, so I'm going to release you but on strict conditions."

Dani nodded.

"Bedrest and hydrate until you're seen by an OBGYN."

"Okay."

"I'll have the nurse come in and go over a diet I'd like for you to follow that will help with the morning sickness. Do you have someone to take you home?"

"Yes." Dylan stepped forward. "I'll take Dani home." He

felt Dani's gaze on him, but he didn't care. He'd make sure she got home safely.

"It was nice meeting you, Miss Clark." The doctor stood; his scrutinizing gaze made Dylan feel uncomfortable. "Congratulations." The doc left the room, leaving Dylan and Dani alone.

"Dylan, you don't have to take me home. Melody's here."

"I know I don't have to. I want to."

~

*A*fter the shock that Dylan had bought a sportscar wore off, Dani slept on and off on the way home. The times she was awake, Dylan was quiet and far away. She had been nervous to tell him that she was pregnant, but going about it like taking a Band-Aid off in one big pull was the best way. She wasn't keeping her pregnancy a secret, nor would she use it to trap Dylan.

Before she knew it, Dylan was pulling into the parking garage. She went to open her door, and Dylan stopped her. "You sit there."

Dani watched him jog past the front of the car to her side. He opened the door, helping her to her feet. Dani didn't protest; she liked having Dylan's full attention.

They made it to the elevator, then to her apartment floor, again in silence. Dani unlocked her door and walked in. She turned around to thank Dylan for driving her home, but he was already in her apartment preparing her couch for her. Dani watched the rocker fluff pillows and clean up her mess from earlier. Who knew Dylan Grace could be so domesticated?

Dani placed her hand on her stomach. The thought of a baby growing inside her was hard to believe, and she didn't know how to feel about it. Was she ready to be a mom? Her gaze fell back on Dylan. Was he prepared to be a dad? Was she doing this alone, or was she doing this at all? No, that last one she knew wasn't even an option. Questions flooded her brain that she couldn't answer, nor was she ready to have that conversation with Dylan.

"Hey." Dylan stood in front of her. "Are you okay?" He looked at her stomach as if what was growing inside her was a monster. She had her answer.

"I'm tired, that's all. I should get to bed. Thank you for driving me home."

"Cupcake, you don't have to thank me. I wanted to."

Inside, Dani beamed when he called her cupcake. She'd missed that. Quickly, she shook free from that emotion. She wasn't falling for Dylan's charm again. "Well, I'm sure you must be busy. I don't want to keep you."

"Are you trying to get rid of me?"

Dani was taken aback. "I just don't want you to think you owe me anything."

He took a step closer. His eyes locked onto hers, and Dani lost her breath. "I'm not going anywhere."

Dani shook her head. "Dylan, you don't have to stay. I'll be fine."

"I'm not taking no for an answer." His tattooed hands gently framed her face. "I'm going to be the best goddamn home nurse you've ever seen. I can fluff a pillow like a motherfucker."

Dani laughed.

"Seriously, let me take care of you like you took care of me, okay?"

Dani nodded, totally speechless and too exhausted to argue.

"Anything you want, it's yours, cupcake. All you have to do is ask."

Dylan walked her over to the couch. "Get comfortable. What do you have in your pantry?"

"Good question." She plopped on the couch. "Crackers."

"Not a problem. I'll fix you something to eat and make you some tea. All you have to do is relax and let this rock god pamper you."

Dani smiled as she watched Dylan make his way to her kitchen. She had to confess, the thought of him taking care of her every need felt good. Really, what woman wouldn't want sexy, lead singer Dylan Grace to take care of them?

Dani lay down and pulled the blanket over her body, pushing away the dark cloud that hung over her. Eventually, they would have to discuss their situation. But not now. Dani snuggled into the warm blanket, relaxed, knowing Dylan was with her right now.

19

*A*fter a week of playing nurse, Dylan needed a break. Alone at his old stomping grounds, he sat at the bar staring at a whiskey tumbler half-filled with Jack. The bar was the last place he needed to be, yet it brought him comfort. He had a love/hate relationship with The Sweet Sin Lounge. The swanky bar had served him well throughout the years. It was full of sexy sin and wild fantasy if you knew the right people, which Dylan had. It had been both a curse and a blessing.

A woman's midnight laughter coming from a booth to the right of him caught his attention. The dark-haired woman in a black mini dress and her rocker guy were nearly fucking. Dylan recognized the lustful look in the woman's eyes. He sensed the thrill of sex in the air. Hell, he'd lived that scenario. Years ago, that rocker would have been him.

The smell of whiskey brought Dylan's attention to the drink in front of him. Even though he hadn't taken a sip, the taste of the amber liquid was familiar on his tongue. Shaking his head, he tried not to think about the past, but the memories flooded back.

Before Gracefall had made it big, Dylan would have done anything and everything to keep his dream alive, even if it meant getting into a relationship for the sole purpose of his girlfriend supporting him. It hadn't taken long for him to realize he'd been played as well. The women who partied at Sweet Sin were looking for something too—to land a rock star.

Broke, horny, and naïve rockers on all different levels partied hard and indulged here. It was easy to target wealthy women who wanted the rock and roll fantasy. It had been perfect. He had not a cent to his name; the chick was wealthy and willing to spend her money on him. That was how he'd been able to afford the leather pants he'd worn on stage.

He'd stuck around for a while until she was sick of him taking up space in her living room and kicked him out. But there was always another one waiting to fulfill their fantasy. And he'd been more than willing to oblige. It was how he'd survived. As long as Dylan could keep rocking with Grace-fall and making his dreams come true, it hadn't bothered him that women wanted to take care of him. Not until now.

Dylan thought long and hard while sitting, trying to fight the urge to drink. His old demons were scratching, threatening to resurface. It would be easy to drink and fuck his problems away. But in the morning, they'd still be there. Maybe if he hadn't met Dani it would have been an option.

"Fuck," Dylan groaned quietly as he scrubbed his hands down his face.

Since he'd met Dani, he'd used her too. But somewhere along the line, he'd fallen in love with her, and as his past stared at him from across the room now, more than ever, he regretted treating Dani like she was some kind of sex toy. The more sober he got, the more he realized how important she was to him and his existence. And now, she was the mother of his child.

Fuck, he was going to be a dad. He let that sink in for a while. What did he know about being a dad when he hadn't grown up with one? The closest person he'd had to a father had been Leo Sterling, Melody's dad. Even with Leo's support, Dylan hadn't been able to shake free from his demons.

"Hey." A warm, comforting hand squeezed his shoulder. "I came as fast as I could."

Relieved, Dylan closed his eyes. Elliot was here.

"That bad, huh?" Elliot sat down next to him, eyeing his tumbler of Jack.

"You have no idea." Dylan glared.

"Oh, I bet I do. We're recovering addicts, Dylan. I get it. I'm glad that you called."

"Yeah." He rubbed the tension from the back of his neck. "I feel like I'm on the edge of doing something stupid."

"Then you made the right choice." Elliot motioned for two glasses of water from the bartender.

"Dani's pregnant."

Elliot fell silent. This wasn't good.

"I know; I fucked up."

"You know, when I found out I was pregnant with Elijah, I was sixty days clean and filing divorce papers. I was scared as hell to be a single parent. I thought there was no way I could take care of a baby when I couldn't even take care of myself. Eli changed my life for the good. He gave me purpose."

"You're a stronger woman than I." Dylan smirked half-jokingly.

Elliot grinned. "Do you love her?"

Dylan froze. He didn't know what love was. "I care a lot

about Dani. She's been my rock."

"You didn't answer my question."

"Look, Elliot, I don't know." Dylan shoved his hand through his hair. "All I know is my world is a much brighter place with her in it, and that makes me feel selfish for wanting her in my life because I'll end up hurting her. It's what I do." Dylan reached for the tumbler.

"If you hate yourself right now, you'll hate yourself even more in the morning if you drink that."

"Fuck!" Dylan pushed the tumbler of Jack off the bartop, and it crashed onto the floor behind the bar. The bartender gave him a sour look, a warning to not start trouble.

"You want to know what I see?" Elliot asked.

"No. But you'll tell me anyway."

"I see what you're failing to see. You're not giving yourself credit. Trust your instincts."

"How am I supposed to do that when I can't trust myself?"

"You're doing it right now. Tonight you were heading into darkness, and you knew to call me. And even if I didn't come tonight, you wouldn't have thrown your sobriety away. I think deep down, you know how you feel about Dani and the baby. You need to trust in yourself because Dani deserves all of you."

Dylan thought about every word Elliot had said. She was right. He was afraid to trust himself, but he trusted Dani. Could he actually do this? Could he give Dani everything she needed and be a father to their baby? "I don't even know how to be a dad."

"Babies don't come with manuals, Dylan. You learn to be the best dad you can be by trial and error. Children are forgiving."

"Well, where I grew up, there wasn't forgiveness. I hated

my mom for choosing drugs over Joe and me, and I hated a father I never knew and all of the assholes she dragged in."

"But you can break that family panorama. You have."

Dylan gazed at Elliot. Again, she was right. This was something he could control. Wasn't this something his psyche had been preaching as well? Whether Dani wanted a relationship or not, he could be there for his child. "You know something, Elle?"

"What?"

"I fucking hate it when you're right."

"I know." She smiled. "Jake hates it too."

Elliot's phone buzzed, and she answered it.

"Hey."

"Yeah, he's here."

Elliot gazed at Dylan and smiled. "Everything is good."

"Will do."

Elliot ended the call.

Dylan knew who had been on the other end. "Dani, right?"

Elliot nodded. "I think you should go home and talk to her. You have a lot of shit to figure out."

Dylan nodded. "Thank you for coming tonight."

Elliot stood and grabbed her purse. "Dylan Grace, are you getting emotional with me? That's so not rock and roll," Elliot teased, making the side of Dylan's mouth curve up into a lopsided smile. "Whatever you do, trust your gut."

Dylan nodded as Elliot left the bar.

He was alone again as he glanced over at the dark-haired woman and the rocker making out in the corner booth. *Fucking pathetic.* He'd been foolish to think that he'd find the answers coming here tonight. Sweet Sin was his past; Dani was his future. Their baby was his forever. So what was he waiting for?

20

*D*ani paced her living room floor, waiting for Dylan to return from the bar. Thank God Elliot had been there. She kicked herself for not having the baby conversation sooner. However, she didn't know what to think. That all changed when she swore she felt the baby flutter. It was too soon into her pregnancy to actually feel the baby move, but the sensation made her want this baby more than anything, regardless of if Dylan stuck around.

Of course, she wanted Dylan in her life. She loved him, but he was her kryptonite. She didn't mistake him for a dream; Dylan Grace was a one-way ticket to the dark side. But she didn't care. She'd follow him wherever together may be. If that was even a place.

Dani stopped mid-pace as she heard her front door being unlocked. Dylan walked in, and she froze. She forced herself to stay planted right where she stood, fighting against the urge to run to him.

Christ, pregnancy hormones sucked!

"Hey," Dylan said as he gazed at her suspiciously. "Are you okay?"

"I should be asking you that question."

"Cupcake, I'm far from okay."

"We should talk about our situation."

Dylan nodded as he laid his car keys on the table and walked into the living room. He sat on the couch and patted the cushion next to him for Dani to sit down.

Nervous and scared, Dani sat on the edge of the couch. "I'm keeping the baby." She placed her hand on her stomach. "You don't need to stay. If you want to leave now and never talk to me again, I'm okay with that. I don't expect you to be ready for minivans and diaper bags. You have a career and fans and I get that; besides, you're still in recovery."

"And you have your career. Why didn't you tell me you dropped out? Mellie told me you had one semester to go before you'd have your master's."

Dani shrugged. "You needed me."

Dylan scrubbed his hand through his hair. He was pissed at himself for not paying more attention to Dani's needs. "I'm going to fix that if you want me to stay." His voice was low and deep and made her heart ache.

Of course she did, with every fiber of her being. However, she knew better than to want something she couldn't have. And the question had always been how long would he stay? Tennessee had proved he could settle down if he wanted to, but did he want to? She couldn't risk a part-time father for her child. Parents that weren't there for their children shouldn't have them, and she knew that better than anyone. She needed to work on herself and finish her master's degree.

"I don't know anymore." She shook her head as she lied to protect her heart. "Every time I think I'm over you, you remind me why I loved you in the first place. I can't keep falling in love with you over and over again just to be rejected. I'm through loving someone who doesn't love me back. And now with a baby in the picture, it wouldn't be fair to them either."

"Dani, you want God's honest truth? I've always wanted you in my life. But every time we got close, I checked out because I didn't want to hurt you. I was too fucked up to care for anyone. The last thing I ever wanted to do was to hurt you."

A tear slipped from her eye. If he only knew how much it hurt to love someone who didn't love you back. "Maybe we're better off apart."

Dylan leaned forward, resting his forearms on his thighs. "Don't say that, cupcake. Please, don't say that."

"Then give me a reason not to." She prayed Dylan would give her that. It was all she needed.

"Fuck," Dylan sighed as he looked up at the ceiling. Was he crying?

Dani reached over and placed her hand on top of his. "Talk to me."

Dylan nodded. "I can do this."

"Whatever you tell me won't change the way I feel about you." Gently, she squeezed his hand, letting him know she was here for him.

"When I was eight years old, before Leo took Joe and me in, I was sexually abused by one of my mom's boyfriends."

Dani squeezed her eyes shut, keeping the tears at bay. Her suspicion had turned into a nightmare.

"He'd beat the shit out me, break me down, then—"

"Dylan—"

"Christ." He wiped the tears falling down his face.

"Was that the same boyfriend that Joe put in the hospital?"

Dylan nodded. "I never told Joe the whole story. I can't. I

can barely tell you." He looked at her, tears streaming down his face. "Please, don't hate me."

"Hate you?" Dani caressed his cheek, wiping a fallen tear. "Why? You've done nothing wrong. You were a kid. You are the victim."

"Then why do I feel like it was my fault?"

"Because that's what abusers do. They manipulate their victims into believing it's their fault. What he did to you was not your fault."

"Maybe not, but the pain is still there. At least when I was using I could numb the pain. Now, I just run. It was why I wanted you to stay away. It's why I push people away. I didn't want to bring you into the darkness, Dani."

"Dylan, you can't find your way through the darkness without a light. Let me be that light for you. Together, we can get through this."

"You really want to do that?"

Dani smiled. "You are so worth it."

Dylan studied her for a moment, and within the silence, Dani saw how much Dylan wanted to move on from his past. There was hope. "I'll spend every waking moment proving to you that I am worth it." He faced Dani, cupping her face. "You're the only woman for me. There's no other place I'd rather be than here with you." He gazed down at her belly. "And our little crumb snatcher."

Dani glanced at her stomach.

"Dani, please let me prove that I'm the best fucking baby daddy in the universe."

Dani looked up and met Dylan's stare. How could she say no? He'd bared his soul to her. He was the one man she loved and who drove her crazy at the same time. She nodded.

"Really?" A wide smile spread across his face, and it warmed Dani's heart and brought her hope.

She nodded again and smiled.

"Fuck yeah, cupcake." Dylan shot off the couch, pumping his fists, celebrating like he'd won the lottery. "Whatever you want, you name it, and it's yours. Back rubs, feet rubs, breakfast in bed, you got it. Designer nursery, strollers, car seat, fucking diapers, you got it." Dylan studied her living room as if he was taking mental notes. "Cupcake, we've got to get on it and baby proof this place unless you want to move closer to your parents."

Dani knew what he was doing. He'd switched gears, done with visiting the darkness. "Dylan, the baby isn't due for a while. We have time."

"You know, I've never met your mom and dad," Dylan pondered. "We'll have to set up a dinner." He took out his phone, looking at his schedule. "Next week?" He glanced up at Dani.

"Dylan," Dani said patiently. "Sit down."

Dylan sat next to her on the couch. Dani took his phone then held his hands. "You need to slow down because you're driving me crazy right now."

"Right. Sorry. I just don't know where to start."

"How about cuddling with me on the couch and watching a movie?"

"I can definitely dig that." Dylan lay back with his arm stretched over the back of the couch. "Come to papa."

Dani shook her head and smiled as she snuggled against him. This was good. He'd finally let her in, and she understood him a little more. Could it be that their baby was the light, the hope they both needed? Could she let her guard down?

Dylan rubbed her arm as she scanned the TV channels for something to watch. "You won't regret this, cupcake."

Deep down, she prayed he was right. "I hope I can survive Dylan Grace high on being a baby daddy."

Dylan put his hand on her stomach and caressed it softly. She looked up at him as his eyes were set on her belly. He didn't have to say a word. He was happy and content.

Dani reached up and caressed his cheek. "I love you." She knew he wouldn't say it back, but he needed to know her true feelings.

He kissed her forehead as he held her tight, and that was enough.

21

*D*ylan sat in Davidson's old office at Cleft Tonic Records. The police had finished confiscating the last of his ex-tour manager's things as evidence that the bastard had stolen money from Gracefall. Dylan hadn't wanted to believe that someone close to him would steal from the band. Yeah, the dude was an asshole; the only reason he'd dated Ash was to drive him crazy. There had been something suspicious about Davidson, but Dylan could never put his finger on it, nor could he talk about it with Joe.

His brother had trusted the creep and didn't want to see what Dylan had seen, a rat. Joe was loyal to the core as long as he didn't get screwed over. Davidson was in for a rude awakening.

Dylan leaned back on the black leather couch, watching Joe pace the office looking like he wanted to murder someone. He knew that look all too well.

The last police officer left with an arm full of files. Dylan didn't want to be here dealing with this shit; he wanted to be with Dani. For the last two weeks, he'd stayed at her place, showing her that he was right where he wanted to be. He took care of her every need, cooked, and as promised, gave the best foot rubs. Every morning he woke up next to her, living for her smile. It was the drug he craved.

Why he couldn't have given her that in Tennessee, he didn't know. But now, the baby, them being a family, made it all right.

But everything wasn't perfect yet. Dani wasn't convinced that they wouldn't end up going back to their old fuck buddy days. He understood. Gracefall was about to go full throttle into promoting the new album, which meant his time would be stretched thin. He wanted Dani there with him so he could take care of her and the baby, but she had a life of her own. Things were about to get more complicated.

Joe sat down next to Dylan and leaned forward, resting his arms on his thighs. He hung his head. "I can't believe Davidson. All these years, I thought of him as family."

"Yeah, the black sheep of the family." Dylan snorted. "Dude, I knew something was wrong with that guy."

"I trusted him." Joe shook his head.

"Don't beat yourself up, bro. Davidson was cunning."

Joe looked up, eyeing a bookshelf filled with signed rock and roll memorabilia. "I wonder how much all that shit cost."

"Sure it was a pretty penny."

"Fuck that." Joe shot off the couch and grabbed a guitar that had been hanging on the wall behind Davidson's desk.

"What the hell are doing?" Dylan stood, confused. He wasn't going to— "Shit, dude!" Dylan shielded his face as pieces of shattered wood flew from the guitar Joe had just bashed into the bookcase, smashing Davidson's prized possessions. Joe went in for another swing, clearing the whole bookshelf and then some.

"Joe, I think you've made your point. Put the guitar down," Dylan warned.

"Holy fuck!" Jake walked into the office, stunned at the destruction. "What the hell is going on?"

Dylan crossed his arms as he watched Joe take out another shelf filled with award plaques. "He's letting out some pent-up anger. Rocker style."

"You do know that guitar was signed by a legendary KISS member."

Dylan sucked in a hiss. "Yeah, I wasn't going to stop him. Go ahead, if you'd like to give it a try."

"Nope." Jake shook his head as he watched the chaos erupt. "I value my life."

"What's going on?" Tyler walked in, ducking as something flew past him.

Davidson's desk flipped over, causing Dylan to take a step back. "Godzilla going ape shit."

"That bad, huh?" Tyler stepped over debris as he joined Dylan and Jake.

"On a scale of one to ten, ten being he's lost it, we're looking at a ten right now. I'm expecting at least an eleven or twelve before it's all over." Dylan continued watching the raging Godzilla.

"I've never seen Joe lose his shit like this," Jake said.

"Yeah, it's not very often we're treated to this side of my brother."

A few minutes had passed, and Dylan, Tyler, and Jake were still dodging objects. There was no sign of Joe slowing down his rampage. A receptionist walked by, sticking her head in. Dylan waved her off. As long as there was no security guard or police threat, Dylan allowed Joe to release his rage.

"Joe?" Dylan turned his attention to the door and saw Melody. Elliot and Dani were behind her.

"Dani!" Dylan strode over to her, blocking her from entering the office. "Don't come in here."

"What's going on?" Dani asked, looking confused at what was taking place. "Did you tell him?"

"No." Dylan looked over his shoulder at his brother completely melting down. "I don't think now is a good time."

"I got this." Melody carefully walked in. "Joe, baby," she said calmly. "Put the chair down."

Joe stopped with the chair in mid-swing. "Mel?"

"Hey." She smiled and walked over to him, instantly calming the beast.

Chest heaving and breathing hard, Joe put the chair down and hugged her. "What are you doing here?"

"I was out with Elliot and Dani, and my dad called saying he needed to meet Elliot here." Melody looked around the office, observing the wreckage. "I didn't know the band would be here."

"Leo called me, too, wanting me and Dylan to meet him here."

"Me too," Jake and Tyler said in unison.

"Mellie," Dylan said as he helped Dani step through the rubble. "What's Mr. Leo up to?"

Melody shook her head. "I don't know."

An awkward silence fell over the room.

Dylan held Dani's hand as he took in what remained of Davidson's office. "Bro."

A look of surprise washed over his brother's face as Joe realized what he had done. "Fuck," he groaned and rubbed the back of his neck. One look at Mel, and the beast was gone.

"Davidson messed with the wrong band, babe." Melody put her arm around Joe. Dylan smiled, as he now understood the bond between his brother and soon-to-be sister-in-law. What he wouldn't do to have that connection with Dani.

Dylan caught Dani gazing up at him. A warm feeling came over him when he looked into her vibrant blue eyes. His world was brighter, his heart was fuller when Dani was around. She felt like a home he'd secretly wished for all these years. "You're looking at me weird again." He gave her a teasing smile.

"Me?" Dani placed her hand on her chest, pretending to be offended. "You started it," she teased.

Dylan wrapped his arm around her shoulders and pulled her against him. "Busted, huh?"

Dani faced him. "I love when you look at me like I'm the only woman in the room."

"And naked." He winked. "I love imagining you naked."

"Take me home, and you won't have to imagine anymore." She flashed him a wicked grin.

Disappointed, Dylan exhaled. "We're waiting for Mr. Leo."

Dani nodded.

"But as soon as he leaves," Dylan squeezed her ass, "your ass is mine."

Dani seductively bit her bottom lip and looked at him with lust-filled eyes, tempting him like the devil. "Deal."

Davidson's old office fell silent as Leo Sterling walked in, overflowing with rock star swagger. Before he said a word, he made his way to Melody and kissed her cheek. "Sugar Plum."

"Hi, Dad," Melody greeted.

Leo then turned his attention to the destroyed office. His

dark-eyed glare stared right at Dylan. "Did you do this, son?"

"No, sir." Dylan shot Joe an *I'm sorry but not sorry* glance.

"I did," Joe spoke up. "I'll pay for all damages."

Leo waved him off. "This is nothing compared to the hotel rooms that have met my wrath." He stepped over a smashed planter of succulents.

"I'm sure you've heard about Davidson ripping us off," Dylan said as he watched Leo pick up an office chair.

"Yes, I know. That's why I'm here." Leo brushed the debris from the chair then placed it in the middle of the room. He unbuttoned his suit jacket, sat down, and then leaned back and crossed his legs as he observed the band members. Dylan recognized that look. Leo wasn't here to take them to lunch. He meant business.

Dylan was confused. Leo had never interfered with Gracefall business. What was going on?

Leo cleared his throat. "You guys have found yourselves in a mess, huh?"

Dylan and Joe nodded.

"And you're kicking off a tour next month?"

"That's if we have the money." Dylan exhaled in frustration. "All our funds are tied up with this criminal case against Davidson."

"Yeah, we don't even know the full extent of the damage," Joe added. "Nor do we have a band manager."

Leo nodded. "I wouldn't worry about that. I happen to know that management has your back one hundred percent."

"And how do you know that?" Dylan asked.

"Son, I own Clef Tonic Records."

Dylan was even more confused. "But I thought Big Rick owned it."

"Nope. Rick works for me. I wanted to be a silent owner and let the talent represent Clef Tonic Records and not my name."

"Did you know about this?" Joe asked Melody.

"No, I didn't." Melody looked as shocked as Joe.

"I signed Gracefall. Not as a favor, but because Gracefall is that damn good. I believe in the band, and that's why I'm stepping in as your new band manager."

Everyone went silent. Dylan didn't know what to think about the God of Thunder becoming Gracefall's manager. He looked over at Joe, who was just as surprised. Dylan then glanced over at Tyler, who was stone-faced.

"Well." Leo stood as if his business was done. "I'll leave you all to discuss." He began walking toward the door.

"Leo, wait," Dylan stopped him.

The rock legend paused and turned to face the band.

Dylan stepped forward. "This is a huge bomb you've dropped."

"Not as big as you knocking up Dani," Tyler interrupted.

Dylan flashed a glare at his bandmate. "What the fuck? How do you know? I haven't told anyone." He felt Dani's hand leave his. *Fuck!* He gazed at Dani and met her heated vibrant blue gaze. "Cupcake, it's not like that. You know I'm all in. I just haven't thought of a good way to break the news to the band."

Dani folded her arms across her chest and rolled her eyes.

"Bro, I'm sorry. I told him," Joe confessed as he glared at Tyler.

"Hey, you know I can't keep a secret."

"Neither can you, Joe." Melody shook her head as she placed her hand on her hips. "I can't believe you told him."

"Mel!" Dani shouted. "You weren't supposed to tell

anyone."

Dylan wasn't shocked. Melody couldn't keep anything from his brother, but he still had to give her shit. "Mellie, I'm so disappointed in you. Tsk, tsk. You broke the girl code."

"Shut up, Dylan," Dani and Melody exclaimed in unison.

"I'm trying to wrap my head around how no sex turned into a pregnancy?" Jake asked, stunned about the news.

"Bro, I tell you, chicks look at me at me and boom, they're pregnant." Dylan felt Dani swat his arm. "I'm joking."

Leo cleared his throat, obviously not amused. "Congratulations, but can we focus here?"

"Right. Like I was saying before I was brutally betrayed." Dylan smirked at Tyler as he placed his hand over his heart as if he had been hurt.

Tyler mouthed "fuck you," which gave Dylan great satisfaction.

"In all seriousness, I can speak for the band when I say we're honored to have a legend such as yourself believing in Gracefall. If it wasn't for you, Mr. Leo, Joe and I would still be living in the trailer park—"

"Or in prison," Joe added. "Don't know what we've done to deserve your love, Leo, but I'll spend the rest of my life proving to you that I'm worthy." Joe gazed down at Melody and held her hand, smiling.

"There's no doubt we want you on our side. Welcome to Gracefall." Dylan rushed over to Leo, giving him a huge hug. Joe and Tyler joined with Jake and Elliot close behind. Dylan stepped out of the hug-fest before letting the emotional moment ruin his *I don't give a fuck* reputation. "Seriously, you all, get it together."

Joe pulled him back into the hug, right where Dylan wanted to be.

22

*I*n her bathroom, Dani wiggled out of the dress she'd just worn to Melody and Joe's rehearsal dinner and slipped on Dylan's black dress shirt. She inhaled, taking in his spicy, woodsy cologne, which did nothing to soothe her raging pregnancy hormones. In fact, it had taken all her might to be a good girl after seeing him in those black dress pants that hugged his ass so nicely.

The whole evening her mind had been in the gutter, thinking about the wicked things she wanted to do to Dylan and what she wanted Dylan to do to her. Seriously, she felt out of control.

Dani looked in the mirror, finger-brushing what was left of her curls. She looked down at her stomach and turned from side to side, noticing a tiny baby bump that only she saw. A smile spread across her face as she thought about having Dylan's baby. A baby wasn't in her plans, but this little surprise was now her whole world. It was still surreal and even more unbelievable knowing that sexy rock god, Dylan Grace was in her bed waiting for her right now. *How did this happen?*

"I think your parents liked me," Dylan said sarcastically from the other room.

Dani cringed, remembering how her mother and father had reacted to the news. Dani hadn't wanted to do the big reveal at her best friend's rehearsal dinner, but her prodding parents hadn't left her much choice. There hadn't been a big scene, though her father had voiced his opinion about what he'd do to a particular body part of Dylan's if he broke his daughter's heart. On the other hand, her mother had been smitten by Dylan's rocker charm. She hadn't blamed them for their shocked reaction. It was the first time they had met Dylan, and they'd dropped a bomb on them.

"Yeah, you definitely made an impression." Dani took one last look in the mirror, then decided unbuttoning one more button on her shirt would get Dylan's attention.

As Dani began to walk into the bedroom, she paused and leaned against the doorframe. Her sexy rocker was sitting on her bed, reclining back against the headboard. Her lustful gaze roamed down his naked tattooed chest to his unbuttoned dress pants. He looked relaxed with his legs crossed at the ankles and a book in his hand. "What are you reading?" She sauntered toward the bed.

Dylan looked at the cover. "*What to Expect When You're Expecting.*"

Dani blushed. "I thought I had put that away."

"It was on your nightstand. Am I not supposed to read it?"

Dani kneeled on the bed and crawled over to Dylan. "I think there are better things to read." She straddled his lap and winked.

"It's actually very educational." He turned the page in the book, continuing to read as she kissed and caressed his neck, trying to convince him to change his mind.

"Did you know right now our little peanut is developing fingers and toes?" Dylan shook his head. "Fucking incredible."

Dani appreciated his research on babies, but she seriously needed to be explored. Her lips left his neck, but she kept her hands on his chest. "Have you gotten to the part about an expecting mother's increase in sexual libido?"

Dylan looked at her as if she'd grown two heads.

"You haven't." She turned her head to the side, eyeing him with a seductive glare. "How about the change in breast size?"

Dylan's eyes fell to her breasts.

"Dylan Grace, I'm shocked," she said as she played with his nipple ring. "Of all people, I thought that would be the first chapter you would have read."

Gently, he opened her shirt and studied her boobs. "Fuck yeah, dude."

Dani bit her bottom lip. "Put the book down and play with me, Dylan." She rocked her hips forward, rubbing her sex against his length through his dress pants.

Dylan tossed the book to the floor, then his hands were squeezing her ass as she returned to kissing his neck. "Are you sure that having sex is safe for the baby?"

"Absolutely safe."

His touch sent her body into a total sex-driven frenzy. Her core throbbed with desire as Dylan slipped his hands under her panties and gripped her ass. Christ, she wanted him. All of him. Now. "I've been thinking about you all night," she said breathlessly between kisses.

"Is that so?" Dylan arched his brow. "What exactly were you thinking about?"

Dani took his bottom lip between her teeth and playfully nipped. "All the places where I wanted you to touch me."

Dylan's hands moved to her shirt, and he finished unbuttoning it. "Tell me, cupcake, where do you want me first?"

His smooth, deep voice sent a shiver down her spine. She gazed lustfully into his eyes. "I need you right here." She took his hand and guided it inside the front of her panties.

"Right here?" Dylan slipped two fingers through her folds, hitting her G-spot.

She almost came undone. "God, yes." Taking in his masterful touch, she leaned her head back. At this rate, it wouldn't take long before he brought her to the edge.

"Christ, Dani, you should have told me sooner that you needed to be fucked."

"Trust me," she said breathlessly, "I thought of many ways to get you alone during the rehearsal."

He slipped his finger inside her, and Dani moaned in pleasure. His lips were on her swollen, sensitive breasts kissing and sucking, which intensified her desire. One thing about Dylan Grace that never changed: he knew exactly how to drive her wild.

Needing more, she rocked her hips forward, inching his fingers deeper. He brought her close to the edge of shattering into a million beautiful pieces when he stopped. "You're not coming without me, cupcake." He pulled his pants down and freed himself.

"I wouldn't dream of it." Quickly, Dani removed her panties.

"Normally, I'd stick with my moto, 'ladies come first,' but you've got me hot and bothered." In one fluid motion, Dani felt Dylan thrust inside her. She gasped.

"Fuck, you feel fucking amazing."

Dani wrapped her legs around Dylan and held on tight as he plunged deep inside her. At this moment, she felt beautiful, wanted, and could she even dare to say loved?

All it took was one hard thrust, and Dani came undone, coming hard.

"Look at me." Dylan cupped her face, not missing a beat.

Dani tried, but her body was no longer hers to control. The best she could do was rest her forehead against his.

"I want you to look into my eyes, cupcake, when I come inside you." Caressing his cheek, Dani looked into his eyes as she still rode the wave of her orgasm. His gaze was intense, burning with desire.

"That's it, cupcake."

She fell into his sensual glare as they both came together. Dylan slowed the rhythm as if he didn't want it to end. Being in this moment, she felt a shift; it was in his eyes. This wasn't about sex. They were sharing something special. Her heart felt it.

Dylan continued to hold Dani as they both came down from the high. Dani didn't want the feeling to end. She cradled his head to her chest. "That was amazing."

He glanced up at her, looking sexy with his *I've just been fucked*, rustled hair. "Fuck yeah, it was. I told you I'd take care of your every need." He winked as he kissed her breast. "I love your new tits. Fucking beautiful."

"Well, I'm glad you found a new play toy." Dani laughed.

"Me too." Dylan rolled over, taking Dani with him. The feeling of the weight of his body on top of hers made her want to go another round. He bent down and kissed her gently. As he rose up, he stared into her eyes. Dani knew what he wanted to say, but he couldn't.

"You don't have to say it, Dylan."

"Say what?"

"That you love me." Dani cupped his face, stroking his cheeks with her thumbs. "I love you."

Dylan looked away. Dani was testing his limit; she prayed that she hadn't taken it too far. "It's okay, Dylan."

Dylan shook his head, then turned his attention back on Dani. "I don't deserve you." His eyes roamed down her body and stopped at her stomach. "Or you, little peanut."

"You deserve to be happy. Are you happy?"

Dylan gazed deep into her eyes as he caressed her cheek. His lips curled into a smile. "I am."

She returned the smile.

"For the first time, I can honestly say I'm happy."

"Good. Let's make a deal right now. Let's promise we'll do whatever it takes to make each other happy, and we'll let each other know when we're not."

"Dani Clark, you have my word. I'll spend the rest of my days making you the happiest woman in the world." He bent down and kissed her. "Trust me, cupcake, it's all sunshine and rainbows from now on." Dylan rolled over onto his back. "And if you want the unicorn, you can have that bastard too."

Dani laughed as she pulled the bedcovers over them. She snuggled against Dylan, and he put his arm around her. "A unicorn, huh?"

"Yep. The brightest and most magical mofo you've ever seen."

"Wow! That's nice and all, but I only want one thing."

"What's that, cupcake?"

She traced part of the raven's wing tattooed over his heart. "Your heart."

He covered her hand with his. "Are you sure? I mean, a unicorn is a sight to be seen."

Dani playfully slapped his chest. "Can't you ever be serious?"

Dylan rolled Dani on top of him. He stared into her eyes, and just like that, Dani was under his spell. "It's yours. All of it."

Tears welled in her eyes.

"Dani, don't cry." He pulled her hair back away from her face. "I didn't mean to make you cry."

"I know. These pregnancy hormones are taking me for an emotional roller coaster tonight. Trust me, they're happy tears."

Dylan pulled her into a hug, holding her against his chest. "Let's just cuddle."

"Sounds amazing." Dani got comfortable and laid her head down on his chest where she could hear his heartbeat. She loved this rocker with everything she had. She loved the chaos he brought, she loved his crazy sense of humor, but most of all, she loved his heart.

23

On the beach, Melody's bridal party was gathered inside the bridal tent, getting ready for the wedding of the year. Four bridesmaids and one maid of honor had been dressed in champagne-colored, spaghetti-strapped, satin tea-length gowns that hugged their bodies perfectly. Two makeup artists and two hairdressers hustled between the bridesmaids making sure everyone was perfect while Melody was being pampered by her own hairdresser and makeup artist.

Dani looked into the mirror. Her hair was down and curled and pulled back by a pink and red lily to one side. Her makeup popped with red lips and smokey eyeshadow, and her skin glowed thanks to pregnancy hormones.

"You look fucking beautiful."

Dani turned around and lost her breath. Dylan was standing next to her, looking rocker sexy in his black tux, eyeing her like he was currently sexually destroying her in his head. She hadn't heard him come in.

"Hey." She smiled and gave him a hug. "You're not supposed to be in here."

"I know." He fidgeted with his tie. "But the view in here is much better."

Dani rolled her eyes.

"Seriously though, Joe wanted me to check on Mellie."

Dani adjusted his tie. "That's nice of you, and you can reassure the groom that his bride is in good hands."

Dylan cupped Dani's face and pulled her into a kiss. Dani's knees went weak.

Someone slapped Dylan on the shoulder. "No kissing the maid of honor. You'll smear her lipstick," the makeup artist scolded.

Dani laughed as she wiped her bottom lip. "You better go before you get us into trouble."

Dylan rolled his shoulders, obviously uncomfortable in a suit. "Yeah, I should get back. Tyler has already started on the champagne. Need to keep him at least standing so he can perform the flower dude duties."

"I can't believe Mel talked him into being her flower dude."

"Right? He hates weddings as much as I do."

"Really?"

Dylan shrugged. "Weddings make me twitchy."

Dani looked around the tent at the hustle and bustle of everyone preparing just for the wedding party to look good. "Yeah, it all seems like too much. My wedding will be on the beach in Morocco wearing a white bikini."

A sly smirk spread across Dylan's lips. "Fuck yeah, dude. Deal. I'm totally down with that."

Dani was taken aback. "Who said we were getting married?"

"Me. I mean, I'm the baby daddy."

"Are you serious?"

"Why wouldn't I be?" Dylan sounded a little offended.

"What did you think, I'd let you marry some other guy and leave him to father our baby? No way, babe."

Dani's thoughts were spinning; she was speechless.

"Listen, I have to get back before Joe thinks there's something wrong."

Dani nodded.

"I'll see you in a few." He kissed her forehead.

And just like that, Dylan Grace left, leaving her dumbfounded. But that's what he did. Never a dull moment with him.

"Dani," Tomi tapped her shoulder. "I think Melody needs you."

"What's wrong?"

"I was taking some behind-the-scenes shots, and she started crying," Tomi explained.

"Okay." Dani tried to keep cool.

"She's over there." Tomi pointed to a sectioned-off area. "She won't let anyone in."

Shit. "Thanks, Tomi." Dani strode over to the makeshift room, praying that she didn't have a runaway bride on her hands. "Melody, honey, it's Dani. Can I come in?"

The door opened, and Melody peeked out. Mascara trails ran down her face. "Oh, sweetie." Dani walked in and hugged her best friend. "What's wrong?"

Melody sat down at the dressing table. "Fucking nerves." She grabbed a champagne flute sitting on the table and downed it. Melody looked at Dani. "I don't know if I can do this."

Dani did a quick time check. "Well, sweetie, you have thirty minutes to decide."

"I know."

Dani knelt down beside her best friend. "What has you second-guessing everything?"

"I'm scared, Dani. I'm scared that Joe and I will end up like my mom and dad."

Of course, she was. Dani had been there with Melody during her parents' ugly divorce. She'd heard all of Melody's childhood stories about having a rock star father and an alcoholic mother. It was no wonder she was a wreck. "Listen, Mel, Joe loves you so much. I've never seen another couple that supports each other like you two."

"I can't lose him." Melody covered her face and cried.

Dani rubbed her arm. "Even if you tried, you couldn't lose Joe. He wouldn't allow it. I'm sorry, Mel, but you're stuck with him."

Melody let out a small laugh.

"You know it's true."

Melody nodded.

"You love him, right?"

"Yes."

"He loves you, yes?"

Melody nodded.

"Love will get you past anything that comes your way. Trust me." Dani placed her hand on her stomach. "I never thought that I'd see the day that Dylan and I would be together, let alone having a baby. If we can do it, you and Joe can most definitely do it."

Melody nodded and wiped her cheek. "I so needed to hear that."

"I know, sweetie."

Melody inhaled a shaky breath and looked into the mirror. "Shit, I messed up my makeup." She grabbed a tissue then wiped her face frantically.

Dani stopped her. "Don't wipe, blot." She took the tissue and helped Melody remove the mascara trails from under her eyes.

"Dani," Melody said. "I don't know what I'd do without you."

Dani gave her a reassuring smile. "Well, it's good that we'll never have to find out. You know I'll be calling you every day on your honeymoon."

Melody laughed. "That won't be happening if Joe has a say so. My cellphone will end up in the ocean."

They shared a good laugh.

Thirty minutes later, Melody's makeup was touched up, and she was looking beautiful, ready to marry the man of her dreams.

Dani waited for her cue as the last bridesmaid and groomsman walked down the aisle. Behind her, Tyler, with his pulled-back, long curly dark hair practiced throwing rose petals from his fanny pack.

"Dani, should I throw like this?" Dani turned around in time as Tyler tossed petals over his shoulder. "Or should I throw them like confetti?" He threw a handful of petals in the air.

Dani laughed. The big, strong-minded, "I don't believe in love" man was nervous. How Melody had talked him into being her flower dude, she'd never understand. "You're just now figuring this out?" Dani kept her voice down so Melody wouldn't hear.

"No." Towering over Dani, Tyler leaned into her and lowered his voice. "I've been practicing for weeks."

"Be yourself."

"Dani," one of the ushers called out. "It's time."

Dani turned back around. It was her time to walk down the aisle.

Barefoot with red polish on her toes, Dani made her entrance, enjoying the cool sand against her feet. The sound of waves crashing to shore and the glow of orange hues hanging over the horizon as the sun began to set was the perfect setting for a beach wedding.

Melody and Joe's family and friends sat patiently, waiting for the beautiful bride on either side of her. And she was stunning in her elegant ivory lace, Boho wedding dress. It wouldn't be long before she'd finally get to see Joe's reaction as Melody walked down the aisle.

Dani took her spot and waited for Tyler to make his grand entrance. She glanced over at Dylan standing next to Joe, and his sexy rocker smile made her blush and her knees go weak. It was still hard to believe that they had ended up like this, in love and having a baby.

AC/DC's "You Shook Me All Night Long" belted through the speakers, and Dani froze.

Oh no!

Dani didn't want to look, but she forced herself. Tyler stood in his tux at the aisle entrance, shaking his hips like a male stripper and tossing rose petals like confetti at the guests. He stopped midway and air-guitared, lip-syncing the song. Dani didn't know what to do. Should she stop him or let Tyler be Tyler?

The guests stood and joined in, dancing and cheering with Tyler like they were at a rock show. Dani dared a glance at Joe to see how he was handling the situation. To her surprise, the usually brooding, unreadable drummer was smiling and having a good time. Dani watched Dylan lean into his brother and say something. Even though she couldn't hear him, she knew a "fuck yeah, dude" was the response. Everyone loved Tyler's dance moves. And Tomi was right there snapping pictures, documenting the show.

The music stopped, and Tyler took his spot, sitting with Melody's mom. Dani had placed him in charge of making sure Mr. and Mrs. Stirling behaved. It was a shock that

Melody's father had brought a date to the wedding when her parents had been getting along so well.

The "Wedding March" began, and everyone stood and turned to Melody. She wrapped her arm around her father's and smiled. Dani held back the tears as the God of Thunder told his daughter that he loved her. Tomi captured the moment.

There wasn't a dry eye when Mr. Leo kissed Melody's cheek, then handed her over to Joe. Going against tradition, Joe passionately kissed his soon-to-be wife. They couldn't be happier. As Joe and Melody took their places in front of the officiant, Dani glanced at Dylan. He looked so ecstatic to be gaining a sister.

The ceremony was short and sweet. Before Dani knew it, Dylan was escorting her to the reception, which was also on the beach. Everyone cheered as the deejay introduced the newlyweds for the first time. They went right into the first dance as the bridal party found their tables. Dani placed her bouquet on the table by her seat, which happened to be right next to Dylan's.

As she watched the happy couple dance, she felt Dylan snake his arm around her waist and pull her against his body. "This is the happiest I have ever seen my brother."

"They look so blissful." Dani laid her head on his chest. "It's not every day that you get to witness childhood friends become husband and wife."

"He's only had eyes for Melody." Dylan kissed the top of her head. "Cupcake?" He placed his hand on her belly.

"Yeah."

"We're going to be that happy. I promise."

Dani faced him and rested her arms on his shoulders, caressing the back of his neck. "That's a big promise to make."

"You'll see." He grinned his sexy rock star smile.

The music stopped, and Joe's voice came over the speakers.

"Can I get my Gracefall brothers onstage?" Joe looked at Melody. "Babe, this is for you." He kissed his bride on the cheek then left for a makeshift stage where the band's instruments were set up.

"Cupcake, I gotta go." Dylan gave her a quick kiss.

Gracefall took the stage as Dani walked over to Melody. "Hey, Mrs. Grace."

"Oh. My. God. You are the first person to call me that," Melody beamed.

"Sounds pretty good, huh?"

"The best." Melody pulled her into a side hug and laid her head on Dani's shoulder as they waited for the band to play.

The music started into a beautiful, heavy melody, but it wasn't until Dylan began singing that Dani's heart filled with love and warmth. His blue-gray eyes were on her the entire time he belted out the sincerest love song. She'd recognized it. It was the same song he and Ash had been working on. She felt a little foolish now. Ash had been helping Dylan, not trying to get him back.

Dylan didn't sing love songs, but he'd done this for Melody and Joe, making him even sexier.

The song ended, and both Melody and she were a sappy mess.

"That was beautiful." Melody sniffled.

Dani reached inside the top of her dress and pulled out a tissue she'd stashed just for this occasion and handed it to Melody. "Blot, don't wipe."

Melody let out a small laugh. "You're the best fucking maid of honor."

"I know." Dani shrugged. "Now go to your man."

Melody met Joe as he was coming off the stage, and he picked her up, hugging her tight.

Dani needed a break from all the overflowing happiness. If pregnancy hormones weren't bad enough, add happy tears, and she was heading straight into an ugly cry. In search of some fresh air, Dani walked down the shoreline. She took in deep breaths as she pulled herself together.

"Did you like it?"

Dani whipped around, and Dylan was walking toward her.

"It was beautiful."

Dylan shoved his hands in his front pockets as he stood next to Dani. They watched the waves crash against the shore. "You want to know something?"

"Sure."

"I'd never written a love song until I met you."

Dani didn't know what to say. "Well, I'm glad I inspired you. Melody loved it."

"I sang the song for Joe and Mel, but I wrote it for you."

Tears welled in Dani's eyes. It was inevitable; she was going to cry tonight. "You wrote 'Beautiful with You' for me?"

Dylan held her shaking hands. "Every word."

"I'm speechless."

"Dani and Dylan. Dylan and Dani," he said as if he was testing the names out. "I like it." He glanced at her, rocking back and forth on his heels. "We're like Tommy and Gina, Jack and Diane. They did it all for love. I guess what I'm trying to say is that I love you, cupcake."

Dani froze. Was this really happening? Dylan Grace loved her.

"Say something." Dylan stepped in front of her. "Did I freak you out?"

"Dylan, I've waited a long time for you to tell me that you love me. I just don't know what to say."

He cupped her face and gazed deeply into her eyes. "Just tell me that you love me."

"I love you." She wrapped her arms around his neck and hugged him tightly. "I love you. I love you."

"Fuck yeah, cupcake." He picked her up and spun her around, then put her down. "I'm going to be the best boyfriend ever."

"Wow." Dani acted surprised. "Not only do weddings make you twitchy, but they also make you sappy. Dylan Grace, are you going soft on me?"

Dylan put his arm around her as they walked back to the wedding. "Baby, there's nothing soft about me, and I will prove it to you later."

"Promise?"

"Promise." He bent down and kissed her. "I love you, Dani Clark."

Dani smiled from ear to ear. She'd never tire of hearing her rocker say those words. Never.

EPILOGUE

The party was getting totally out of hand, and Dani found it hard to breathe as people packed into the hotel. The music was loud, the alcohol flowed like a river, and the chicks were half-naked. It was the last night of Melody and Joe's honeymoon, and they had invited their closest friends to Las Vegas to celebrate before the guys went back on tour. Word about the party had gotten out because she was sure that Melody didn't know half of these people.

Yet, Dani sat on the couch with legs draped over Dylan's lap, claiming her man in front of the line of women chomping at the bit to sneak in and get a taste of Gracefall's frontman.

Not tonight, bitches.

He was kissing her neck, rubbing her bare legs, and Dani loved every minute of it. While her best friend had been off on her honeymoon, Dani had felt like she was on her own with Dylan all to herself. He'd stayed with her as he closed on his house in Malibu, which wasn't too far from Melody's place. He'd told her that the six-bedroom, six-bathroom, Mediterranean-style house had once belonged to a legendary rocker. Dylan hadn't given her a tour yet but reassured her the shark tank had been removed from the kitchen and the yellow fur-lined room had been remodeled. However, the sex swing was still debatable.

Dani closed her eyes, losing herself to Dylan's touch.

"You want to get out of here?" he whispered in her ear.

Hell yeah, she did. Dani nodded. "But this is Mel's party, and I don't want to be rude and leave."

Dylan slid his tongue up her neck, and Dani changed her mind. Rude didn't seem so bad.

"I don't think she'll notice that we're gone. Looks like she's busy." He tipped his chin, and Dani followed his gaze toward Melody and Joe, making out on the other side of the room.

"Yeah, you're right." Dani caressed his cheek. "Your place or mine?" It was a silly question since they were sharing a room, but God, how she loved to tease him.

"My place."

"Your place?"

"Yep, I need to show you something. Give me ten minutes to make a call, and we'll be flying back to LA."

"Dylan, it's late. Why don't we leave in the morning like planned? I'm exhausted."

"Because the timing is right. Besides, you can sleep on the plane."

Dani loved his spontaneous nature, but it was hard to keep up. "Okay."

"I love you." He kissed her quickly and stood. "Meet me back at the room in ten."

Dani nodded.

"I'll send Mac over to make sure you make it out of here alive."

"See ya in ten."

Two hours later, Dani was off the plane and sliding into a Bentley. She buckled herself in as she waited for Dylan, who was conversing with the driver. Dani wondered what was going on, as Dylan had been fidgeting through the whole forty-five-minute flight.

Dylan got into the car. The driver left the tarmac and took a wrong turn onto the highway.

"Where are we going?"

He leaned over and kissed her. "It's a surprise."

"I love surprises, but it's three o'clock in the morning. Don't you ever sleep?"

"I'll sleep when I'm dead." He gave her a sexy smirk.

It wasn't long before Dani recognized the area. "We're driving by your place?"

Dylan nodded.

Dani shook her head, wondering what he was up to.

The gates opened, and the driver took them up the driveway and parked the Bentley in front of Dylan's new home.

"Wait here." Dylan got out and again conversed with the driver.

The suspense was killing her.

Dylan opened her door and she got out. "Is this my surprise tour of your new place?"

"Kinda."

Dani followed him through the courtyard to the arched front door. She got a glimpse of the neatly trimmed shrubbery and small palm trees through the landscape lights. Dylan unlocked the door and walked inside, eagerly flipping a switch to illuminate the room.

Outside lights shined through the windows, revealing

just how many there were. Fresh paint and clean air rushed Dani's senses as she took in the massive area.

"So, what do you think?"

Speechless, Dani looked around. From the glossy, white, marble-tiled floors to the black, wrought-iron staircase to the spacious foyer that opened up to the enormous pool area, Dylan's place was extravagant, just like him. "It's beautiful."

Dani followed Dylan into another room. "In here is your study or room or whatever you want." Wall-to-wall cherry wood bookcases framed the room, and in middle sat a huge matching desk. Dani walked over to the desk and took in the computer set, which looked like a command station from a spaceship. What had he done? "Dylan—"

"I wasn't sure what you needed for school, so I kinda got one of everything."

"Are you serious?"

"Yeah, I thought once you were done with school this could be a place to start your own business. I can see it now. Chaise lounge over there by the window for your patients. Dr. Cupcake name plate on the door. And, by the way, you have a meeting with a Professor Johnson on Monday to get you back in class."

Dani was stunned. How had he pulled that off? Probably rock star charm. "I don't know what to say. Thank you."

Dylan smiled. "Anything for you. I have something else to show you." He started up the stairs, and Dani followed, taking in every detail of the home. They walked down a wide hallway to another foyer, which was small compared to the one downstairs. He opened a set of dark wooden double doors and let her in.

"This is our love nest." Dylan wrapped his arms around her waist from behind, and he nuzzled her neck with kisses.

Again, Dani was speechless, and not because of the size of the suite, which was completely furnished and decorated, but because Dylan had said this was *their* place.

"There's more." Excitedly, Dylan led her to another room right off the master. Dani looked in and lost her breath. Tears welled in her eyes as she took in the crib, changing table, and rocking chair. "What did you do?" She walked over to the crib, which was decorated in neutral colors. She smiled as she picked up a stuffed music note pillow, then held it to her chest.

"I had everything painted neutral, but once we find out the gender, you decorate however you want."

"It's perfect."

The sound of something jingling caught Dani's attention. She suspiciously glanced at Dylan.

He tipped his chin to the bedroom. "Go check it out."

Dani placed the pillow back in the crib then walked into the bedroom. She was greeted excitedly by a Blenheim Cavalier King Charles puppy wearing a pink collar. She bent down, and the puppy jumped into her arms. She was the cutest thing Dani had ever seen. When she scratched the pup's neck, she noticed a key hanging from its collar. She looked up at Dylan. "What is this?"

"Figured you'd need a key to your new home and someone to keep you company while I'm on the road. And a study buddy."

Dani stood as the pup licked her face. She couldn't believe everything Dylan had done for her. This was huge. "You want me to move in with you?" she asked for clarification.

"I do." He leaned in and got a kiss in before the pup. "There's more."

"More?" Dani couldn't keep up.

"Cupcake, there's always more with me." His sexy, crooked smile made her knees weak. She followed him to the king-size bed, knowing what was happening next. And to be honest, she never wanted Dylan as much as she did right now.

On the bed was a white box with a red ribbon on top. Funny, she hadn't seen it there before. Knowing Dylan, she had a good idea of what was in the box. "You know lingerie is a waste of money. I never wear it long enough for you to enjoy it," she teased.

Dylan grabbed the box. "I can take it back."

"Don't you dare." Dani set the puppy down then snatched the box.

The box was light and felt like clothes as she shook it. She opened the top, and inside was a brochure of Morocco and a white bikini. Her heart raced as she looked at Dylan then back to the brochure. With shaking hands, she flipped it open and gasped. Two tickets to Morocco. Tears welled in her eyes again.

"So, want to get married?" Dylan pulled out a black velvet box and opened it.

A huge diamond ring stared back at her. Her hand flew over her mouth, stifling a gasp. Was she still on the plane dreaming? Any minute now she was going to wake up, right?

"Dani, you've shown me what love can be, and I want to spend the rest of my life loving you and our baby and killer here." He looked down at the pup pawing his leg. "Jack and Diane, Tommy and Gina, right?"

It was more like Pam and Tommy, but either way, she'd take it. "Yes." She shook her head. "Yes, I'll marry you."

Dylan crushed her into a hug and kissed her even

harder. Dani had everything she'd ever wanted and more. "You know what this means?"

"That you're one lucky cupcake who's marrying a rock god?"

Dani laughed. "Melody will be my sister."

"God, help us all."

"It won't be that bad. You have enough rooms here," she teased.

"Whatever makes you happy."

"You make me happy, Dylan Grace."

Passionately, he kissed her, giving her a promise of what was to come.

Dani had herself convinced that being in love with Dylan would end up a tragedy, but how wrong she had been. It was a love story and a happy ever after. She had the man of her dreams, a baby, and her life back.

"I love you, Dani Clark."

Dani didn't think that her heart could swell much bigger, but it did. Hearing those word from Dylan was all she needed. "I love you, Dylan Grace."

About Victoria Zak

Victoria Zak is an internationally bestselling author of historical and contemporary romance. She weaves magic into her timeless tales, reminding readers anything is possible, especially with a dragon by your side. Raised in Dunedin, Florida, the sister city to Stirling, Scotland, no wonder she grew up fascinated with anything Scottish. Add the ocean into the mix, and it's easy to see where Victoria found inspiration for her stories.

As a child, she read anything she could get her hands on, which developed into full-scale book addiction by adulthood. Curious by nature, Victoria doesn't shy away from anything. She enjoys historical research and hanging out at the nearest coffee shop. Victoria currently resides in Maryland with her real-life heroes, her husband and two children.

Victoria loves to hear from her readers. You can connect with her through the links below:

www.victoriazakromance.com
victoria@victoriazakromance.com
Newsletter http://bit.ly/1uebjmR

facebook.com/VictoriaZakAuthor

bookbub.com/authors/victoria-zak

instagram.com/victoriazakromance

twitter.com/VictoriaZak2

BOOKS BY VICTORIA ZAK

Graceful: Vicious Love Tour Series

Rock Me to the Top

Rock the Line

Rocked and Bothered

Been Caught Rockin' (2022)

Guardians of Scotland Series:

Highland Burn

Highland Storm

Highland Fate

Highland Destiny

Highland Hope

Highland Unleashed (2022)

Ember Brooke Series:

Scorched Hearts

Hearts Under Fire

Daughters of Highland Darkness Series:

Beautiful Darkness

Deadly Darkness

Wicked Darkness

Stand Alones:

www.ingramcontent.com/pod-product-compliance
Lightning Source LLC
Chambersburg PA
CBHW020613180626
46810CB00007B/2758